Twelve dead children. An ex-priest with the faith to move mountains. A hunter out of the depths of legend. Together, they must find a way to overcome their pasts and become something entirely new if they are to defeat an ancient evil.

David Shaughnessy was content in his life as a police detective in Armata, California. It lacked the visceral, sick thrill that came with exorcising demons, but it was better for him, saner. Until the night he got called out to a vicious murder in the woods, and met Dallan Jaeger. The older man and Interpol agent is much more than he seems to be, and their connection is immediate, powerful. Trust blooms quickly as they learn to work together to pursue the evil fae responsible for the murders.

They must learn to do more than trust each other if David is to fulfill his birthright and claim what was so long denied him. Only then do they have a hope of catching the killer...in the Twist.

Copyright 2016 by L.A. Stockman

Published by
NineStar Press
PO Box 91792
Albuquerque, New Mexico, 87199
www.ninestarpress.com

Warning: This book contains sexually explicit content which is only suitable for mature readers.

Print ISBN #978-1-911153-99-3
Cover by Natasha Snow
Edited by Elizabetta

IN THE TWIST

The Wild Hunt

L.A. Stockman

Dedication

To Karen, Bran, Nessa & Bowen, whose support has meant everything when it comes to getting that next word written.

Author's Notes

Since the story takes place in California, the narrative uses US English spelling; however, the main characters are from Ireland and Europe, so UK English spelling is used in their dialogue.

Part One

David

Chapter One

Hanging in the tree, the boy's body looked unreal. A forgotten Halloween decoration, the gore so over-the-top there was something almost cartoonish about it. Yes, David Shaughnessy thought, except for the smell. He wrapped his inadequate suit coat more tightly around his tall, lanky frame and stood in what he was already thinking of as "the viewing circle"—a ring of seemingly random detritus that formed a perfect vantage point from which to view the dead child.

His long-fingered, elegant hands were jammed unceremoniously into his pockets, twitching to make the gestures of faith that he was not entitled to perform. *Dear God, if You have any love for the lost, take this child in Your arms. Forgive his petty, childish infractions and grant him Your most blessed peace.*

That the boy was a runaway was obvious to him: David could see past the fetid, swollen ropes of intestines arranged in elaborate patterns in the branches, the odd way the tree itself seemed to have taken hold of slender arms in a wrap of branch and twist of vine that was not natural, but couldn't really be man-made. There were needle tracks on those delicate arms, clothing that was tattered and torn, and a sweet, thin face just barely introduced to shaving beneath the rictus of pain and fear.

"How long have you lived here again?" The woman's voice came from behind him, to the right toward the parked line of emergency vehicles. "And yet here you are, at oh-dark-whatever-the-fuck in the rain without a proper coat and boots. Shaughnessy, you're fucking hopeless."

"Ellen," he responded quietly, without rancor. The older woman was just trying to help him, take him under her wing. She had a son not much younger than David. How to tell this ruthless pragmatist of a crime scene supervisor the truth? That standing in the cold rain, feeling it chill down to bone and marrow, was the most insignificant of penances, his discomfort a tiny drop of what this child must have felt. It was not right, that he was standing here, having avoided the same fate as the boy in the tree. "I was in such a hurry, I forgot again. Oh, please be careful of this ring. I'll need it carefully documented."

"Right," Ellen said, tossing him a glare as she picked through the clearing with her sensibly attired team armed with flashlights until they found places to set up the harsh spotlights.

David stepped out of the ring and blinked. The scene became palpably less clear to him as the light of his pocket flashlight was swallowed by the rain and predawn darkness. The light didn't quite reach to the boy in the tree, and all the details that were so distinct became dim in the distance. A shiver raced down his spine, and he knew it had little to do with the cold and damp. His hand went to the small intricate silver crucifix beneath what had once been a nicely pressed and starched dress shirt.

In the absence of that clarity, he was forced to move closer to the powerful stench, but he willed himself to put it away, to bear witness without blanching. It was the least he could do for this lost boy. The very, very least. An absent request brought a ladder over, and he leaned it somewhat haphazardly against the tree before clambering up it to look more closely.

The boy was no more than thirteen, perhaps fourteen and excruciatingly small for his age. David shined his light to the boy's face and almost fell off the ladder. Amidst the filth and rain, the small features were composed: eyes carefully closed; face washed clean; wet, dirty hair raked back and some attempt made to untangle it, probably with fingers. There were flowers woven into his hair, flowers that smelled sweet this close, pure and white in the middle of this late-winter muck of rain.

Someone had tried to help.

David was still staring, processing what this could possibly mean, when a gruff, accented voice cut through the background noise of the crime scene team and coroners. He almost fell off the ladder again, but the owner of the voice steadied it with a foot braced against the bottom rung, driving it deeper into the soft earth. "Lad, you're gonna end up on your arse if you're not careful."

"Um, thank you for that...astute..." There was no point in being rude, especially since the unidentified man was correct. "Yes, thank you." David peered down at the man but couldn't make out much thanks to the damnable mist and the man's very weather-appropriate hat. He summoned his few shreds of dignity and climbed down the ladder to face the newcomer. The stranger was older, perhaps in his late forties, with the sort of face that was kind and predisposed to smiling. David found himself staring into warm, gray-green eyes, rapt, and the cold seemed to seep out of his bones.

"I'm Detective David Shaughnessy, Armata Police." If the words fell automatically from his mouth without his brain's awareness, it thankfully didn't show. The instant attraction made him stand straighter, pull his feelings in tighter, and throw up a wall so fast that it almost took his own nose off. "I don't remember calling out for any assistance. The case is only two hours old."

"Dallan Jaeger. I'm with Interpol." Jaeger reached into his breast pocket for his credentials, and handed them over to David.

"This would be California, sir." According to the very proper-

3

looking credentials, this man outranked him by orders of magnitude. "Forgive me, but I'm not sure why you would be here in the general sense, much less here specifically. In the here and now, at this crime scene." *David, you sound like an idiot.*

If he sounded like a fool, Jaeger did nothing to betray his own feelings on the matter. "Nothing to forgive. I was in California already. We've been working with federal law enforcement to catch a serial killer who does...this." He nodded to the boy in the tree. "This is the twelfth victim."

Twelve was one of those numbers, the kind that was never the end of the count. Thirteen disciples, a baker's dozen. Twelve should always be the end, but it never seemed to be. David managed to keep that much inside his mouth as he handed back the credentials. "Twelve? Twelve dead children and this is the first we're hearing about it?" Twelve more mangled bodies. Twelve more souls lost to cruelty and perversion.

"You don't know because we want as few people as possible to know," Jaeger said softly. He turned his head to the side to study David's austere features and the icy-blue eyes that turned an already pale face to a somewhat damp and waterlogged alabaster. The scrutiny made David, if not uncomfortable, then at the very least flustered. "May I?" He nodded toward the ladder and took out his own pocket flashlight. It was not lost on David that Jaeger waited for his nodded permission before climbing up the ladder.

He held the base, because it seemed to be the thing to do, and because it provided the best vantage point to watch Jaeger's examination. One thing he'd found about working in law enforcement—how an investigator approached a victim spoke volumes about how they approached the job. About the quality of the human, and the passion of the professional. Jaeger's hands were as gentle as David's had been, and David heard Jaeger speaking softly in a language he recognized only because of his overabundance of education and voracious appetite for any kind of knowledge. Old Norse.

Then the timbre of the syllables took on a different tone and cadence. It was like hearing someone in the Church today use Latin, compared to how Latin had been pronounced in the ancient Roman world. Or maybe the difference between Italian and Roman Latin. Only, of course, this wasn't Latin at all, and he was only sort of sure it was Norse to begin with.

It was a coping mechanism, this endless go-round of analysis, this restless darting of his mind and making of connections that had nothing to do with the matter at hand. A failing, because he should only be focused on the boy in the tree.

"Shove over a bit, lad?" came the soft question from just above his head. While he'd been gathering wool, Jaeger had finished and was almost all the way down the ladder.

"Oh. Oh! Sorry." David got out of the man's way and offered a hand off the last rung. Jaeger took it without needing it in the least. The man radiated vitality, and he certainly did not need scrawny young whelps to help him off ladders. Those hands probably built barns or something in their time off. "Where did you learn to speak ancient Norse?"

"Where did you learn to recognize it?" came the immediate rejoinder, and Jaeger gave him a look that penetrated just a bit too deeply.

"I read." If that sounded a tad defensive, it was only because people were always and forever asking him how he knew things. The answer went far beyond reading, but it had become shorthand for the protracted, winding, and exquisitely painful road that had led him to this city in Northern California, so far from home and the faith he'd tried to leave behind and failed. So. He read.

"I like a well-read man," Jaeger murmured, the words almost disappearing into the misting rain and the oppressive atmosphere of the surrounding woods.

David had to ignore that, because he was surely interpreting it incorrectly, and refocused on the gruesome matter at hand. "You should see this, sir. It feels very formal, was definitely constructed, and it seems to have a ritualistic purpose." He led Jaeger to the viewing ring and pointed out the detritus of the woods laid out in a circle that somehow transcended randomness into some kind of pattern he couldn't quite see. "If you step inside…"

Jaeger did, and sucked in a breath through his teeth. "Holy hells." His jaw clenched, and he narrowed his eyes, staring at the boy in the tree much as David had a few minutes ago. He squatted down and ran the very tips of his fingers across the edge of the circle, not quite touching it. David blinked several times. It glowed as Jaeger's hand passed over it. No matter how many times he blinked, the glow remained, a sickly green light barely visible but undeniable.

"Sir…" David felt what little color there was in his face fade as Jaeger stood, no creaking joints or popping noises with him, and pulled the sick light up with him, gathering it up into a ball in his hand to study more closely. "Sir…what…" A wave of nausea swept over David with vicious tidal pulls in every direction at once until he wanted to scream or shove or put his hands over his ears and sing "lalala."

Only one thing did that to him.

David forced himself to lean in closer to Jaeger. "Sir, what kind of demon is it?" The whisper was for Jaeger's ears alone.

"Demon?" Jaeger pressed his lips into a line and then squeezed his hands together, and David watched the green slowly becoming suffused with a lambent gold/silver/amber undulating color that was warm and comforting, the light of hearth and home. When he opened his hands, it drifted away into the woods. "Not a demon, little one."

"Don't lie to me. You're not from Interpol. You're from Rome." David's hands formed fists, and he shoved his arms around himself in an almost angry protective gesture. *Did they have to intrude on this, too? Even this?*

"No, lad, I'm from Interpol. I'm not a Christian, much less a Catholic." Jaeger was studying him again, expression gentle, but this time it made David's hackles rise.

He knew how he must have looked, but no demons. Not here. Not again. And no more bullshit from Rome. And yet, if there were one thing he could say with certainty about Dallan Jaeger, it was that his words were true.

"We need to talk, little one. I had to catch a ride out with Forensics. Do you think you could take me somewhere we can speak freely?"

"Yes, sir. And..." David's lips pressed together, reluctantly parting for the words. "Please do not call me that. I am not... I do not like it." *Little one* conjured memories as if by witchcraft that, like so many others awoken this waiting-for-the-sun morning, were hard to ignore.

"My apologies, David." Jaeger meant it. Some people apologized just because it was the thing to do, but Jaeger apologized as though he genuinely regretted any harm he had caused. "You're a professional, and this is your scene. But we cannot do anything else here right now. Let's get coffee, hm?"

Yes, being given a proper direction was very helpful when David felt lost, as he did right now. He nodded and turned from Jaeger, acutely aware of those eyes on his back as he wound his sodden way back up the slight embankment, and then through the now-marked path to where they'd set up a mobile headquarters near the road. Armata may not be the size of San Francisco to the south or Seattle to the north, but they knew how to run things properly, efficiently, and generally quite effectively. One of the many reasons he and Saoirse, his sister, had chosen the place to settle after years of drifting from Rome to Ireland and points in-between.

"David." Woolgathering again, and caught at it like the naughty schoolboy he'd never been. Jaeger's voice was kind, and its depth was a way to center himself in this maelstrom of ugliness and things-best-left-in-the-past. "This is yours, then?"

Unerringly, Jaeger had found the hybrid SUV and stood by the driver's side door, holding it open for David to crawl in. Head pounding from that sick, unwholesome green glow and the nauseating taste of it, of the darkest of the dark, David took several moments to rub his eyes and his temples before starting the truck and pointing it toward town, where the first light was making a valiant attempt to penetrate the gloom.

Chapter Two

Jaeger sat in silence, though the ride was more than half an hour. His scarred and strong hands were clasped patiently in his lap, his stillness a welcome relief to the rabbiting-around of David's mind.

In the half an hour it took to reach a small cafe, just opening for the early commuter breakfast crowd, he'd managed to find something resembling a center, a still place that allowed him to go through the motions of opening the door for Jaeger, and requesting a quiet table and a pot of tea with his usual, slightly befuddled politeness.

David stripped off his soggy suit coat and draped it over the back of his chair, while Jaeger had left his hat and overcoat in the truck. He was wearing a hand-knit woolen sweater and jeans, with heavy, big boots that looked more like something one would wear to war. Or something equally violent.

"My eyes are up here," Jaeger teased softly, a hint of amusement coloring the deep timbre and rolling vowels.

"Oh! I just... Your boots. Sensible for...the woods." David bit his lip and curled his spidery fingers around the mug of tea that had been delivered in his mental absence, as a frenetic warmth crept over high cheekbones.

"The woods...not what you were going to say, was it, David?" As if Jaeger knew. "Why didn't you at least put on a pair of wellies before going out to this mess?" Softly.

"I don't think..." David was suddenly aware he must seem an

idiot to this incredibly attractive man. "...about myself, when I get call-outs. I ought to have, it would have been helpful."

"Oh, but you do think, and you don't miss much. I don't think you miss anything, as long as it's not related to your actual well-being." Jaeger's voice was pitched low, just for them, and it must have been obvious the blush had achieved new heights right up to the tips of his ears.

If this was the most intimate conversation he'd had with anyone not Saoirse in years, then surely Jaeger couldn't tell that, too. "No, that wasn't what I was going to say. Those look like boots you'd wear to war."

"So very close. David, why did you think I was from Rome? And while we're at it, you aren't pissing about with how much you hate them, are you?" Considering that David had almost flown into a rage, it was not as deep as some of Jaeger's other observations.

"I think you must know why." David's eyes darted around briefly. "That was a demon, did that to the boy." When he didn't pay attention, David's accent slipped back to the poor house on the wrong side of Dublin. "Nothing else in this world like that feeling. When I worked for Rome, they sent me out to deal with such things."

"Gods below. Sending you out there with... It wasn't a demon. Or maybe if it helps you to think of it as a demon, it serves well enough." Jaeger drank his tea for a moment, looking like he was trying to figure out how to explain all of this to David, who was too smart for his own good and too tenacious to let it go.

"'Serves well enough...' No. Accuracy matters. Well enough is not good enough." *Spoken like an academic through and through.* "Tell me."

"A faerie called a Sluagh—or so I think, gone mad."

"I know how it feels." Because faeries? He'd heard more

outlandish things, but not by much.

"I can't bloody corner the damned thing, and it's about to reach its trooping ground, and then I'll have to wait another year to give chase. How many more will be taken into the other realm and killed just like those other boys?" Only, with time the way it is in Faerie, each of those deaths would feel as though it took weeks. Months. "This is my last chance. And yes, I am actually with Interpol, just not a branch that deals with the mundane."

Already anticipating David's questions? "A...a Sluagh. A faerie." His tongue darted out to touch his dry lips, and he shook his head, short hair growing ever more fair as it dried in the warm cafe. "Jaeger... I don't know how to deal with a faerie. I'm fairly sure those are just stories."

"But you believe in demons because you believe in your god and your devil and your church and your own eyes." At the words, David nodded. Empirical evidence was hard to refute. "Well, I hate to tell you this, but the Sluagh was here first, and it answers to no devils, no gods."

"Then how can you possibly capture it? How can we make one iota of difference here? How can I bring a bloody faerie to trial and put it in jail? On death row?" David laughed mirthlessly. "Did you know about me, what I used to do, before you came here?"

"There was a note in the file, David. 'Detective in command of investigation: Former priest, former exorcist. Treat with care. Keep out of the way.'" Jaeger was watching David's face as he seemed to go somewhere else, somewhere deep and dark.

"Treat with care. So that I don't get in your way." David was fairly certain that having to cut an infant out of a pregnant woman possessed and beyond saving, to allow that child some chance at life, could not translate into *treat with care*. "If you're right, I will find it, and I will put it down." Sluagh, demon. Faith moved mountains, and that he still had aplenty.

11

"I never said I agreed with the notes, lad." Their little corner of the cafe grew warmer, a small perimeter of amber light springing up from the socially responsible reclaimed-wood floorboards. "Exorcism is not for the weak." Even if it took such a terrible toll on a soul already strained to breaking.

"Can anyone hear us right now?" David's eyes flicked to the light, certain that the two of them were the only ones in the cafe who could perceive it. At Jaeger's headshake, he nodded slowly. "Tell me what I can do, besides running interference at the station."

"The first thing you can do is look me square in the eyes." Jaeger reached out to patiently untangle David's fingers from the tea mug, taking one hand in both of his and rubbing his thumb gently across the thin skin of David's wrist just inside the shirt cuff.

David froze at the physical contact and found he could scarcely breathe around the raging confusion of need that coalesced where the calloused pad of Dallan's thumb stroked his wrist. That he didn't yank his hand back was already a minor miracle. Anyone save Saoirse or the kids touching him generally caused an immediate and brutal reaction as fight-or-flight instincts kicked in. Typically more fight than flight. Not this time, not now.

"Your eyes, David," Dallan murmured, and David complied without knowing why, realizing too late that the maddening thumb was gently tracing up the path of an ugly, poorly healed vertical slash. Dallan locked their gazes and looked far too deeply.

David wasn't sure whether to scream or cry or drop down on his knees between the man's thighs the way he'd been taught. It was worse than seeing him naked, seeing all his scars, all his marks, to have him touching David there.

Jaeger held the moment, held David in place as if pinned, until a surge of raw will, directed through a faith so deep it was like its own suicide scar on David's soul, almost knocked Jaeger on his ass, and certainly made him let the hell go.

"Do. Not." David shook his head, picked his cup back up like a shield, and clutched it in a death grip. He was old enough, now, to make them stop.

"Gods-damn, you have juice, you have balls, and you have brains. Fuck the notes, you're in this with me. I'm not putting you on the bench." Jaeger shook the pins and needles from his hand. "And for the record, I was not doing what you think I was doing."

Oh, no. Not...not a come-on. A test? Somehow he managed to pass even if he thought the questions were written in Latin instead of Greek. Or Norse. "Sorry." Sorry that he'd misinterpreted, or sorry that it wasn't a pass? *Oh, David, you idiot. There is not comfort to be had in either option.*

"Don't be. I should have known better than to touch you unless you give me permission. But now I know."

"You know I'm not some clueless, powerless child you need to keep out of the way? Well, that's reassuring." It was not unusual for expending magical energy to make David jittery and often inappropriately aroused. The latter usually just exacerbated the former and he ended up at downright cranky.

"I know you're an ally." Dallan's lips twitched the tiniest fraction as his nostrils flared for a moment, as if scenting things that David would really rather keep secret.

Or, if secrecy wasn't an option, distracting would work, too. "In an hour or so they'll have the boy laid out in the morgue, and we can examine him. Do the Sluagh leave traces when they kill? Anything we will need to obfuscate?"

"Not to mundane senses, no. But you'll know. You'll smell it." Granted there was a lot to smell when it came to this particular corpse, but nonetheless. "I'll show you." The tone was so intimate that David's heart skittered around alarmingly in his chest at the things Dallan could show him.

"Swear to me that if I bring you into this, if I back you, we'll put this creature down." David had let the mug go free in favor of clutching his hands painfully hard together, knuckles white with it. He had never had to compromise his police work with his other talents, and the thought of missing something concrete because he was off chasing bloody faeries made him feel sick.

"I swear to you, lad. By every old god, I swear." Dallan's voice was different, again, and this time it sounded as though he put a seal on something. A working, a magic. No...an Oath. In the old sense, in the sense that breaking it was unthinkable to a man of honor.

"I accept." Softly. He'd known this man two bare hours, and that was a strange fact-but-not-fact. Of course it had been only two hours. Of course it had been forever. He could swear that he'd heard that voice saying those words in his ear before, a swimmy mess of time and life and long, miserable years bereft.

There was a beat, another, and then Dallan nodded slowly. No mind that David was still a raw nerve quivering across the table, he let the circle fade back into the floorboards and flashed the waitress a charming smile after beckoning her over. "The sign on your door promises the best pancakes in town. I think I'll have to find that out for myself. More tea, too, please. David?"

"No, thank you. Just the tea, please." David couldn't look at her, which he knew was horribly impolite. He'd leave her a huge tip.

After she'd gone, Dallan tutted at him. "You need to eat."

"And you sound like my sister. You can ask her. I'm a lost cause." He paused. "I eat at home in the evening with her and the children."

"You have children? Or she does?"

"We do. We've adopted children, and we take occasional high-risk fosters." The abused and neglected and abandoned.

Dallan shook his head slowly. "I would make a joke about going for canonisation, but I think you might deservedly smack me for it."

"We're no saints, Saoirse and I." Restless fingers unclenched and David tapped rhythmically but quietly against the table. "Come to dinner tonight and see."

"You don't make that offer easily, do you?"

"No one else has ever had the invitation, so I would have to say no." No one that he worked with, no friends. Saoirse had a few friends, but even so, they almost never came to the house.

"I would be honoured, David."

David jerked his eyes away from Dallan, suddenly afraid that he could see too much, too quickly, and spoil everything.

Thankfully, the food arrived, and David could watch Dallan attack it with the kind of enjoyment that had always frankly mystified him. It was hard to tell under the bulky sweater, but Dallan looked solid as an oak tree, and that was not something David had any business considering.

However, since Dallan was wholly preoccupied with the carbs and meat and ignoring the fruit cup, David did feel somewhat justified in reaching in and plucking out a piece of melon, and then another, catching the small smile that Dallan offered as permission. The smell and taste of it went wrong in his mouth, growing to rotten flesh and the smell of demon and gutted little boy. *Stick to your tea.* And again, there were Dallan's eyes, not judging, just noticing. Just paying attention.

Just accepting.

Chapter Three

Within the hour, David and Dallan were back in the truck, and David was silently steeling himself, putting on his "work face." He disliked police culture, as a general rule, and how loud and crude most of them were. Not bad people, not in this city, but still. He felt perpetually like the bookworm trapped in the changing room with all the jocks.

After he got Dallan signed in and fitted with a visitors' badge, he did have to duck into the actual changing rooms, grabbing clean clothes from his locker and slipping into a bathroom stall to change out of his still somewhat damp suit. There were the usual catcalls and teases, but David let them slide around him. What would they say if they actually did see him? The bookworm with so many, many scars. Claw marks, bites, burns, and those cuts, of course. Not to mention the tattoos. Sometimes it made his lips quirk when they called him a priss or a prude or, occasionally, a sissy or a fag. The last was rare; the captain could take some teasing among her people, but not that kind of nonsense.

What would they think if they could see? How green would they turn? How would I choke on their pity?

David changed into trousers, a dress shirt, and a lightweight, sky-blue merino sweater, forgoing the suit coat and tie. Considering he was built, as Saoirse put it, like a deranged spider monkey, his sister had taken to tailoring most of the clothes he bought so he wouldn't look ridiculous in them. Partly, David suspected she wanted him to look well-turned-out because she wanted him to just date someone already. Find a nice boy. Bring him home. Be happy. They both knew why that was not ever going to happen, but Saoirse did her part. She always did her part, did her best, for her brother and all her other lost ones.

When he came back to meet Dallan at his desk, the man did eye him up and down before wrenching his eyes away. "Colour suits you," he murmured as he stood to follow David down to the basement medical examiners' offices. The blue of the sweater did bring out his eyes quite dramatically, or so Saoirse had said. On the whole, he preferred to hide.

"This won't grow more pleasant with procrastination," Dallan said softly.

"No, I expect not." In fact, every time he went down these elevators, David had to white-knuckle against his instinctive fight reflex. It wasn't that he found death abhorrent itself. No, the rage came from the fact that innocents had paid, again, for greed and lust and cruelty, and that there was no one handy to smite for it. Nothing in that room to exorcise. Just a horribly, horribly broken little boy.

Dallan said nothing, but David could feel an answering tension that only increased when they entered the swinging doors. The body was simultaneously tiny and grotesquely enormous, laid out on the cold steel table in the cold room, a thin sheet ineffectually hiding the child's gutted midsection.

"Poor sweet lad," Dallan murmured, leaning in to pull the sheet down. Since the sheet was making a horrible situation yet more horrible, David was grateful.

"We have an hour before the coroner comes in to start the autopsy," David said, pulling a tiny digital camera out of his trouser pocket for photos. It'd be easier to just use his phone for all of it, but the kids loved to play on it.

"That should do." Dallan flicked his eyes up at the security camera, and David could almost hear the fritz and frizzle of it going out. Once they were as alone as they were likely to get, Dallan pulled a few items from his pockets. "Hand me that metal bin right there?"

David did so, dividing his attention between what Dallan was doing with the bin and his own work with the corpse. David put on gloves, and he held one of the boy's hands, scraping gently under the worn-down nails. He gathered whatever he found onto a sheet of paper for transferring into an evidence bag. "Sir, I couldn't help but notice, once I got close...someone cleaned him up. Do you see?" The filthy blond hair was still carefully finger-combed back from the agonized face.

"I do see. Someone couldn't stop it, so they tried to help as best they could. Possibly another faerie..." He shook his head. "No. They don't care for lost human children enough to do this, not even the supposed Seelie Court. Some other wood spirit, sprite, or elemental. If it saw, perhaps we can convince it to talk."

"Huh. Just go to the woods and ask nicely, then?" David collected the flowers from the boy's hair into another evidence bag, sniffing them carefully. "It's a couple of months late for yarrow in these woods."

"Well, for some value of 'nicely.'" Dallan finished mixing ingredients in the bin, and the resultant sudden stench rivaled that of the corpse on the table. It smelled of bog and swamp and rot and unclean things that squelch and cling and suck.

"That is...that's Sluagh, isn't it?" David asked, feeling the too-familiar roil of magic in his gut and pressing hard behind his eyes.

"Good lad." Dallan pushed up the sleeves of his sweater past the elbow, revealing corded, muscular forearms, and then dipped his hands in the mixture, taking care to rub it in so that it wouldn't drip onto anything and contaminate it. "Now watch... If a Sluagh has touched the boy, it will resonate with what's on my hands, and we'll have our proof that we're on the right track."

David stepped back from the body and crossed his arms, watching intently though the smell was making him pale with the effort not to vomit. Dallan's hands slowly, patiently traveled just above the boy's ravaged flesh, starting from the top of his head. Nothing. Nothing where the flesh had been washed clean. "Do...you think that he was touched there, and whoever cleaned him up removed the taint?"

"I think you're exactly right," Dallan observed. "David, can you open his mouth for me a bit?"

David nodded and gently used his blue-gloved hands to lever the boy's jaws apart. Rigor hadn't set in, so he held them, even when Dallan dipped a fingertip inside again careful not to touch the body, and it started glowing with that marsh-gas sickliness. In case there was any doubt, the spell showed clearly enough that the Sluagh had used the boy. *As if torture and killing weren't enough.* Silently, Dallan moved down, carefully navigating around the ropes of entrails. All glowing the unclean color.

The longer the spell lasted, the more the resonance caused David's back teeth to grind, but he kept his mouth shut, focusing on the process, ignoring the mounting pressure in his head and the bile rising in his throat. He would keep his shit together, he would, he kept repeating to himself. *You've seen worse, you've seen worse, you....* But while he had of course, technically, seen worse, he'd never felt any magic like this before.

"Gods, David..." Dallan was just straightening up from between the boy's legs, finally finished, and when he looked over at David again, he blanched. "David. Listen to me, lad. I want you to back out of the room, through the doors. Don't turn your back on me. Then sit on the bench directly opposite the doors. Do you hear me, lad?"

To disobey seemed strangely unthinkable, so David did

exactly as Dallan said, holding the man's eyes until the doors closed and he slumped onto the bench, eyes open and staring as the dissonant hum in his head tried to wipe out his thoughts.

An eternity passed before the doors opened once more with Dallan striding through them, somehow clean again and with a handful of supplies, right up to David to squat between his legs. "David. David, look in my eyes." He cupped David's head with big hands and held it steady. Then he put his forehead to David's and placed a warm hand over each ear.

It wasn't until he did that that David realized he was bleeding out of both ears. Not only that, his back, oh God above, it ached. Like it always did, along his spine, over his shoulder blades, but much worse, an acute pain instead of a chronic throb. David shuddered violently and bucked a little, but Dallan refused to let him go until the hum was finally, blissfully gone.

David let his head fall back exhaustedly to the wall, breathing shallowly at first and then more deeply. Dallan let him go so slowly it spoke of reluctance. *Like he wants to kiss it better*, a traitorous voice in David's head unhelpfully supplied.

"Too bloody right," was the barely perceived response, just before Dallan's hands were gone. "Let's get you cleaned up, hm." He'd brought gauze and antiseptic from the morgue, and used them to clean the blood off David's slender neck and the delicate flesh of his ears.

"I'm sorry I…I seem to have overreacted." David allowed Dallan to fuss over him, because it was soothing and a very appropriate way to let the man touch him. And it helped. Dallan helped with…his mess.

"You're a pure soul, David. You're a beautiful soul, and a beautiful person, and what I called up in there was the antithesis of everything you are." Even David could pick up that Dallan's words were unplanned, that he was going to say something else and that came out instead.

What could he say to that? David laughed softly, mirthlessly, and shook his head. "I wish you were right." Pure, holy. He'd never been enough of any of those things. *Abomination.* "Did you at least see what you needed to see?"

"I did. Did you see enough?" Because obviously this investigation would go quicker and more smoothly if both of them were completely convinced.

"Saw, felt, smelled, tasted, heard... I think we covered all five senses and a couple extra." David nodded slowly, head pounding in rhythm to his heartbeat. He tottered to his feet, legs shaky as he tried to get his bearings on the way to the big metal sink where he could wash his hands and face.

"We won't be able to do the work on this case here," Dallan said, keeping close as though to catch David if he lost his balance.

"Well, no. Sir. I need to go upstairs and finish the preliminary report, deliver it to the captain, and then invent some reason why we'll need to be away from the station so much." And he'd better come up with something convincing. David rolled his eyes at himself; three years here, and he was still the queer foreigner trying to get himself taken seriously.

"Or, you know, the fact that I'm technically in charge of the investigation may help a bit." Dallan smiled and tapped the badge still in his pocket.

"It will, but I still have to work with these people after the case is solved and you're gone," David murmured, acutely aware of how close Dallan was once they got into the elevator. There was a clench in his belly when he said "you're gone," but it was good. Good to remind himself that no matter his regretfully intense attraction, this man would not be here for long. He would not ever be part of David's life, of his family's life. He'd come for a purpose, and when that was fulfilled, he would be gone again, and David could go back to being numb.

Numb was preferable to this. Surely. He'd thought he'd taken his malformed desires out behind the woodshed and put them out of his misery years ago. A lifetime ago.

"Point taken. I'll follow your lead, David." Dallan held the door for him when the elevator opened onto the bull pen, and then followed him into the captain's office.

Captain Ishiguro was in her early fifties, her dark hair just beginning to gray in attractive streaks and bound into a severe knot at the nape of her neck. There was a shelf behind her of awards, medals, and honors. Everyone expected her to retire soon, but David knew better. Somehow he knew that she would never walk away from this job; she would be carried out of it in the back of an ambulance. He hated it when he knew things like that. Hated knowing her fate, and hated more that he was so utterly sure of it.

"Captain, I've come to deliver the preliminary report. Have you met Chief Inspector Jaeger?" Dallan extended a hand, and Ishiguro rose to take it in a firm grasp.

"I have not. The first I heard about Interpol's involvement was when your superiors called me at three AM to inform me of the arrangement you have with the FBI to pursue this case." If she was at all put out by being woken up for work at three in the morning, it wasn't in her voice, or her face.

"Apologies, ma'am. We had to move very quickly to preserve the scene and determine if it is our killer." Dallan spoke respectfully—obviously aware he was on her turf, stealing her best detective, and taking over a volatile and gruesome investigation.

"No apologies are required. Just catch the person responsible. We all want the same thing, do we not? Justice for that little boy." She sounded like she would much prefer the "justice" to be meted out via the business end of her service pistol.

"So, the preliminary report..." David felt unbearably rude, as if he were breaking into a conversation between his elders, and yet he had his own job to do. He described the scene in perfect detail, omitting the supernatural aspects with the sure knowledge that even if she were to believe it, there would be no point in destroying her whole view of creation, five-plus decades of learning how things are supposed to be.

It was the only kind of lying he was good at—lying to protect innocents from knowledge that would hurt them.

By the time he was done, the captain's lips were sealed in a thin line. "And you say you have eleven more bodies across Western Europe and the Eastern US?"

Jaeger nodded. "Yes, ma'am."

"Then I expect there will not be a thirteenth." She was speaking directly to Jaeger, and Jaeger accepted her charge, because that's what it was.

"I would die before I let that happen, ma'am." Again, the weight of those words.

"Let's sincerely hope it does not come to that. Now go on, do whatever it is you people do in Interpol, and bring my detective back in one piece." It was a clear dismissal, and David walked out of her office, bemused, and headed toward his desk. Dallan was following, and of course he was.

Everyone was staring at the newcomer and boggling a little that low-voiced, effeminate David seemed to command so much respect from him. "Look at that...like a puppy," Bismark muttered to her partner, who shook his head.

"More like a wolf, that guy." It seemed to matter little whether David and Dallan could hear them or not. David was used to the teasing, but he was surprised that Dallan let it go.

After David sat down and pulled up his written reports and Dallan sat down to wait for him with a stack of photographs and handwritten notes in a thick leather folder he kept for his own eyes, the murmurs died down, and everyone went back to David's comfort zone—ignoring him thoroughly. His fingers flew across the keys, and he tabbed between one report and another form and something he had to look up on the Internet, and in a shockingly short period of time he was done. Files were put in the proper places on the server, neatly organized with the corresponding photos he'd taken; requests were made with Forensics for a report on the detritus under the boy's nails that he'd sent down via intra-office courier; and a note was sent to the coroner to notify him immediately, please, as soon as the autopsy was finished.

"Right smart at all that bureaucracy, aren't you?" Dallan said softly, the corner of his lip turning up in a smile.

"Have you met the Roman Catholic Church?" David answered, feeling a real smile start to creep across his bitten lips.

"Not if I can help it," Dallan teased good-naturedly.

David's smile was slight, but he felt it actually reach his eyes. On a night like this, that was something of a miracle.

"Do you have a place to go, where we can work? I have a hotel room, but..." Dallan shrugged. "I'd rather not have to hang out the do not disturb and tack horrible pictures all over their walls like some kind of bad film noir."

David sat back in an office chair clearly not ergonomically designed for someone with his height and proportions, his legs splayed out in front of him. "I...do. But you must promise something. I need another one of those oaths of yours. You will be as careful with this space, with my home, as you would be with your own."

"You're going to have quite the collection of my oaths by the end of this, I fear." Dallan leaned forward, eyes serious. "You have my word, David. My solemn word."

Again, it was all David needed to hear to stand and gather his laptop, bag, car keys, and cell. He texted on it while walking, neatly avoiding obstacles, and simply sent to "Saoirse": Incoming. Bringing a friend.

Chapter Four

The Shaughnessy home was, if nothing else, sheltered. At the edge of town, past the last neighbors by a quarter of a mile, it had a tall, faded-blue fence with a suspiciously modern keypad PIN lock. Past that barrier, a path half as long through a riotous garden of vegetables and flowers and herbs led to the sprawling cottage. It wasn't like something out of a magazine. It was whitewashed and already fading, with brightly colored door and window frames in cheerfully clashing shades of blue, yellow, orange, and red.

A wide porch of weathered boards overlooked a play structure with swings and a slide and a pirate's nest lookout. A big well-worn picnic table painted cobalt blue with huge yellow flowers of varying degrees of skillful execution sat close to the swings and the flower garden. The porch was cluttered with rocking chairs and sand tables and easels and toys causing a bit of an obstacle course to the front door.

Unlike most cottages built around the time, there was a second floor. Farther on from the house was another lower gate leading to the bridge. David saw Dallan stop still just down the path, before the steps to the house. A slightly mischievous smile curved David's lips, and he made a gesture with his hand. Dallan shot him a look that was equal parts amusement and regard before he was able to step onto the porch.

"Sorry about the wards." David was very much sorry-not-sorry. He'd poured a copious amount of blood and sweat into those wards, and it was gratifying to see that he'd done well. A stranger with magical abilities could not enter the house without him allowing it specifically.

"Don't be. They're very skillfully crafted...and they cast a hell of a wide net." Nothing, good or ill, could get in here unless it was possessed of the sheer force to brute-overpower the magic.

"Everything precious to me in this world is in this home. And I know that a white hat doesn't automatically equal trust." David opened the screen door for Dallan, and there was music coming from the back of the house, melancholic, yet with a core of hopefulness that couldn't be completely extinguished. David turned to him, actually touched him, pressing his hand against Dallan's broad chest. "Promise me I'm not making a mistake, Dallan."

Since it was David who did the touching first, and no one was bleeding, Dallan laid his own hand gently over David's. "I swear it to you. I will always swear it to you, lovely one. There is no malice in my heart for you or yours. There are only things you do not know yet, but you will. Just as there are things I do not know about you, but I will."

"In the fullness of time," David whispered, because it sounded right, like something out of a story.

"Yes."

"You can't be real." This time, the whisper was little more than an exhalation.

"Feel my heart beat." Strong, steady under his palm. David's world focused down on the thudding beat, and he unconsciously leaned in, mouth drawing closer to Dallan's. "David. If you kissed me now, how would it end?"

David's quick mind turned over a dozen possible outcomes, all of which made him move back in a jerky motion and fold his arms over his chest. "Not well. I... First, I made the assumption you'd want to kiss me." And who would want that? He was the original used bill of goods.

"That was not an incorrect first premise from which to work, but this isn't a classroom." Dallan reached out slowly to unclench David's fists and smooth his arms down from his self-defensive posture, gentle and tender.

"Is it not?" David allowed Dallan to touch him, move him, though it made him want to cry and scream and shove and pull the man so close they lost all room to talk, much less think. "I rather feel that this is exactly a classroom." Or a crucible.

"You aren't ready for these lessons." Dallan pulled his hands back and dropped them to his side. "Soon. Not now."

Suddenly they both became aware of a third presence in the room—a tall, curvy woman with David's blonde curls and blue eyes, body lush where his was spare, dressed in running clothes and trainers. She wasn't moving, just watching, eyes full of what had just happened between her brother and this stranger in their house.

"Saoirse, this is Dallan. Dallan, my sister." David expected to feel embarrassed to be seen touching Dallan, but he didn't. *Because touching him doesn't feel shameful.* A slow, knowing smile crept across his sister's face.

"I've only known David a few hours, and yet he's spoken of you often," Dallan said, as though he'd not just been caught one hairsbreadth from kissing her brother senseless. He walked to her and offered his hand, and she took it.

"He's sweet like that," she replied. David knew his sister well enough to recognize that it was also a warning.

"I'm learning as much." If Dallan picked up on the warning, he obviously accepted it with good grace from the smile on his face.

David's eyes flew between them, anxious, because oh fuck, what if they hated each other? "Dallan is on temporary assignment from Interpol. We're working this last case together, the one I got the call-out for last night."

"Ah, yes. The mysterious call-out." Saoirse tilted her head. "Bad one, then." They were all bad, of course, but some had a shattering impact on David, and she was the one who typically picked up the pieces.

"Fucking terrible," David admitted, and Dallan quirked a brow. "Worst I've seen since I left Rome."

"Shit. I'll put the kettle on, then. Jen's been watching Viva while I went running, so I'll send her on and then make some sandwiches, too, yeah?"

David nodded absently and followed her into the kitchen, where a young woman with snake bite piercings and forest-green hair was holding a little girl of three on one hip. As soon as she saw David, the child held out chubby fists and declared, "Davey!" It was just that, more a declaration than a request, and David smiled as Jen transferred her to his arms.

"Viva, were you good for Jen?" David smiled under the onslaught of kisses.

"I WAS!" Everything with Viva was a very vivid exclamation, because fast-forward was her only speed. She fisted her hands in David's sweater, and then looked over his shoulder at Dallan, dark eyes widening.

Jen laughed and shook her head. "She was hilarious, as usual. I have classes, or I'd stay and give you the third degree about the handsome stranger." She kissed David's cheek and then Saoirse's, and slipped out the back door without waiting for an introduction.

Saoirse put the electric kettle on and started getting out sandwich ingredients, laying them on the butcher block, seeming to spare barely a thought as to what her hands were doing. "You'd better introduce Viva before you have to change your sweater, love."

David carried her over to Dallan and turned so the little girl could see him properly. "Viva, this is Mr. Jaeger. Can you say hello?"

"HELLOOO!" She waved at him, and then hid her head in David's neck and looked at the stranger sideways. Her dark hair was braided back out of her way, and she was wearing jeans and a plain red T-shirt.

"Hello, sweetheart. You can call me Dallan. I don't mind." He waved back and smiled, and David was acutely aware of how he looked, totally unprofessional, a kid on one hip, and making tea with one hand.

"I'm VIVA!" she insisted emphatically. She shifted her weight till David put her down and then sidled over to Dallan.

Dallan crouched down and grinned. "So I heard. Very nice to meet you." He offered her a hand, and instead of shaking it, she gripped it like a lifeline.

"Viva's been with us for almost a year now," Saoirse said, putting together a sandwich for the little girl first, cutting it in fourths and adding some fresh carrots on the side.

"And Jen was the first foster we had after moving here. She's in nursing school and has a flat with her boyfriend. Nice guy. He's good to her." David's tone was clear; this boyfriend had been checked out with every method at his disposal, mundane and magical. "You'll meet Rhian later; we adopted her as a newborn in Rome."

"UP." Viva pointed to her seat at the table, and Dallan scooped her up and situated her with her plate and a sippy cup of milk that Saoirse handed him.

"Ah, a veteran I see," Saoirse teased him, and Dallan laughed and nodded his head.

"Guilty— I've raised a few of these m'self." That made Saoirse raise an eyebrow and look over at David, message received. Dallan seemed to be in his mid to late forties, nowhere near old enough to have raised a passel of children.

"After lunch, we'll need to go upstairs. I'll make sure the door's locked..." David assembled himself a cheese sandwich and ate it over the sink.

"But I'll keep the troops down after school lets out. Dallan, you're staying for dinner?" It was not so much a request.

Saoirse had the ability to fluster people, even people older than her, without trying. This time, Dallan shifted from one foot to another. "David asked me already, so... I hope that's all right?"

"David asked you?" Her eyebrows went north, and she looked at her brother. "I'll be damned. In that case, I'm afraid I'll have to insist."

"All right, we can take the food upstairs." David felt a burning need to diffuse this situation before it reached its maximum sibling embarrassment end state. He kissed the top of Viva's head and then grabbed plates and glasses of water before leading Dallan upstairs.

"I feel like I just met my sweetheart's mum. Been a while since I had that feeling." Dallan chuckled and took the water and sandwiches from David when they reached the top of the attic stairs, ascending one more level until they were at a door, plain, white, heavy old wood. The spellwork laid into it was easy to see. It would be surprising if anyone in the house who was completely mundane even saw the door was there, it was so thoroughly warded.

There was a corresponding door opposite that would comprise the other half of the attic that was completely normal, not a lock to be seen, painted midnight blue with carefully constructed glitter constellations. "That's the studio. Saoirse does most of her work in the workroom out back, but this is for crap weather and keeping bored kids busy. Unfortunately, I need a place to work where the kids won't be tempted to enter. Even Saoirse stays away." David placed his hand in a very precise spot on the unmarked wood, and the door swung open at his touch.

The room beyond was spartan but lovely, with a row of windows on the western wall facing the ocean, just a short walk past that second gate. The first thing David did when entering was to open all of them and let in the sunshine and breeze. The floors were old scrubbed wood, with a large protective circle carved into the middle of the room, easily five of David's paces across. It was the magical equivalent of a bomb shelter, big enough to put everyone in the house inside if needed. The rest of the room was dominated by a desk that ran the length of the north wall, and a battered but comfortable sofa.

"Right... You don't ever feel safe, do you?" Dallan murmured, taking it all in, walking the perimeter of the circle of protection, peering at the runes glittering back into his eyes with a faint silver.

"No." Simply. There were reasons and reasons, but as he'd said earlier, they would just have to wait.

"What sort of runes are these, David?" Dallan's voice was still soft, but David could hear the tinge of sadness. Not pity, at least David knew that now, but sadness. And curiosity.

"The ones I know. The ones I've always known. They work, and that's what matters." He paused, standing by the desk with a mini-USB cable in one hand, his camera in another. "Do you recognize them? I haven't shown them to anyone else who...well, who..." The words wouldn't come, but the meaning was clear.

"Not even your church?" Dallan looked up at him, head turned to one side as he crouched to run his fingertips across one of the intricate carvings.

"Especially not them."

"David...they're angelic runes." Those sea-green eyes watched him, watched his face, searching for a reaction that David wasn't sure how to give.

He forced himself to finish plugging the camera into the photo printer, and then started the parade of grisly images. He flipped open the lid of his laptop and powered it on. There was nothing else to do until the technology caught up, and there was Dallan, standing close but not too close, waiting for him.

"Then…I did well by not showing them what I could do," he finally replied softly. "I worked most exorcisms by myself, and was very successful, but I threw away their rule book after my apprenticeship was over. I used these words, these symbols, and they worked. Better than Latin or Hebrew. How do you know what they are? I thought…you had nothing to do with the Roman faith."

"I don't, but my people remember when they were made, those angels, that god, dreaming up his own little hegemony and peopling it to suit him, shutting out the rest of the world. And when those angels of his fell… My people remember the chaos, the misery, and the death."

"I suppose I was just born knowing." David had a nice, impenetrable brick wall between himself and those trains of thought, and he wasn't ready to breach it now, not when there was so much work. "Can you access the Interpol files on the previous victims? I'd like to set up a map."

Dallan said nothing more, but he moved to take one of the two chairs at the desk, the one in front of David's computer. "Theoretically, but I'm rubbish with these things." He opened a web browser, pulled up what seemed to be a very official field operations site, and then entered a username and a lengthy password. Which failed. "Bugger."

"You don't have to try to go fast." David rested a hand against Dallan's shoulder. "Just peck it out, no extra points for speed."

"Like I want you thinking I'm some out-of-touch old man," Dallan muttered, pecking out the lengthy string of characters again, apparently flustered by David's light touch.

"Never. I have a feeling that you catch onto the basics very quickly." Because it was so very obvious that computers were a new thing to him.

"I'm mostly bollocks at typing." Those hands were made to hold reins and bows and swords and small children and baby farm animals, not to tap on bits of plastic.

"Me looking over your shoulder's not helping, is it?" David smiled and squeezed said shoulder, the muscle solid under his palm. It was only then he realized he was touching at all, and he took his hand away.

"'Fraid not. Performance anxiety."

"I somehow doubt that." David turned away and gathered the printed photos and a box of thumbtacks from the desk and began to arrange them on the wall. *Was I just flirting? I was just flirting. Bantering about performance was definitely flirting.*

"Got it." Dallan sounded endearingly proud, and David went back to his side, this time pulling up the spare chair to sit next to him instead of hovering. "We started all the way back in Pforzheim, in the Black Forest."

The folder contained pictures of another boy, this one dark haired and lanky where the one in Armata was blond and compact. "Kids that age...so much wild deviation in body types and growth patterns. He was the same age, right?" David reached past him to zoom the image onto the boy's hands.

The dirt under the nails was fresh and wet looking, and while the nails were tattered from a struggle, the cuticles were neatly kept. "Not a street kid?"

"No... Pietr's mother had to stay late at work, and he was walking home from football practice. It's a safe route; he'd walked it a hundred times without incident. Only this time, he caught a monster's eye." Dallan's voice was level, but hinted at more information buried. Or something he didn't want to say.

"I think... Let me see, Dallan." David tugged the laptop toward him and started opening all of the folder links in new tabs, looking at the pictures quickly, and he saw what Dallan didn't want to say. "They were all attractive."

"Our Sluagh certainly thinks so," Dallan muttered, appearing uncomfortable with assessing the physical beauty of children. It was another in his ever-growing list of deeply attractive qualities.

"It's all right," David said, fingers twitching with the desire to put his hand back on Dallan's shoulder. "I'll crawl in, so you don't have to. You've been at his heels six months. Let me think like a monster for a while. I'm used to it."

"I would have spared you this, had I known." Dallan pushed back from the desk to let David work. He was immediately pulled into the files, eyes scanning rapidly, giving no indication he'd heard Dallan's low murmur.

He'd heard, but David hadn't the words to respond. Spare him? If he'd known what? *He can't possibly know about that. Please, God above, don't let him know.* It was easier, for opposite-world values of easier, to dive into the case. Now that he had more data, more context, more pieces, his quick mind latched on as though the investigation was a safe port on a particularly stormy sea.

His eyes are exactly that colour. That grey-green of a storm that is so great and terrifying it pulls up all the ocean's secrets to toss them about like toys.

David shook his head hard and reached for a drink of water, blinking, and printing out certain pictures and files. Not all of them, not all of the statements of the parents and friends and hapless discovering strangers, just some.

As documents and photos emerged from the printer, Dallan took them and arranged them on the wall without comment, and without guidance. If David was just repeating all the work that he and his Interpol colleagues had done, the other man wasn't saying so.

The reddening of the light as the sun began to set marked the passing hours, accompanied by distant commotion when the rest of the kids got home from school and the cacophony of several musical instruments being practiced at varying stages of proficiency. As the soundtrack for a life, it was wonderful.

Clearly, it was also so commonplace that none of it stirred David except that he muttered under his breath once, "Nailed the *F* above high *C*...good girl..."

Just before dinner, David felt he finally had a handle on the case up to this point. "So the cleaning of the latest boy's face and the flowers in his hair are the things that are utterly unique to this case."

Dallan nodded from his place on the sofa. "Like I said, I think it was probably some sort of forest spirit that did it."

"Do you know how to make forest spirits come out and answer questions?" David put down the last file folder and turned in the spinney chair to face the older man.

"That I do, lad. It's best done at dawn or dusk, so we're a bit late for tonight. We should go in the morning and see what we can find. She must have seen what did this. Where it went."

"She? Is that universally true?"

"Not universal, but pretty damn close to. They reproduce through magic, and the few males you'll find—stag lords and such—tend to be more into each other."

"Ah. I suppose that makes sense." David stretched, and his shirt rode up for a second before he tugged it down. "I should take you down to meet the rest of the horde, and then change before something unspeakable gets on my good sweater."

"I'd like that very much." Dallan stood, eyes going to the bare patch of skin in the split second before it was re-covered. "They sound like quite a group, at least from up here."

"You could certainly say that." David's lips quirked. "We have a tendency to collect the unusual. The ones who are rejected for being too much, too strange, too different." Because if anyone would know how to relate, it would be David and Saoirse.

David slipped out of the workroom and held the door for Dallan before sealing it again behind him. "Viva's our youngest, but Rhian was our first. We...we got her as a newborn."

On the second floor they passed a bathroom full of kids washing up for dinner. "Shh, if we're very careful they won't notice us," David stage-whispered, and got mobbed for his trouble, just as he'd intended. Viva headed straight for Dallan and demanded, "UP," while a golden-haired beauty of a little girl came to hug David. She clearly demanded pride of place among the pack of children, and she was packing an enormous amount of magical power in her slim frame.

"Dallan, this is Rhian. And Oscar and Arthur." Arthur and Rhian were both nine, but he was as different from her as could be, with dark skin, close-cropped hair, and very serious glasses. Oscar was sixteen, and wearing eyeliner and lip-gloss along with chipped purple nail polish. "Everyone, this is my friend Dallan. We work together, and he'll be staying for dinner."

"Will he read us a story after?" Rhian asked, looking at Dallan with her head cocked to one side.

"Well, for one, that's quite presumptuous, and for another, it'd be more polite to just ask him yourself, love." Rhian moved with a feline grace toward Dallan, who had Viva on his hip in the hallway, freeing David up to give hugs to Arthur and Oscar. Oscar was enthusiastically going on about a new show at his school and how he was totally going to nail the lead part this time, and Arthur told him about some impossibly high grade on an algebra exam.

"Will you, Dallan? It's always story time after dinner, and I would very much like it if you read to us." Rhian was definitely uncanny in some way, but it was hard to put one's finger on precisely how.

"I'd love to. What are you reading right now?" He shifted Viva around and the three of them went downstairs to the main floor together.

"*The Hobbit*. I love it! I want to be like Gandalf when I grow up."

"I don't blame you, he's very powerful."

"Yes, he is! I want to be powerful so I can be like David and take care of everyone." David touched Dallan's shoulder from behind, cutting into the conversation as though it was a dance he'd stepped through many times before.

"You'll be you, my love, and that's more than enough." David skirted the topic of the blonde-haired nuclear bomb he had under his roof. He knew there would be a reckoning one day in the not-so-distant future, and everything about his family could change in a heartbeat with one decision from Rhian.

Once downstairs, the conversation was forgotten. It was spaghetti night, and everything was delicious, and every one of the Shaughnessys was delightful in their own way, even quiet Arthur, who spoke up when it mattered and said brilliant things.

Chapter Five

David was waiting outside the gate when Dallan pulled up in a rental SUV at five the next morning. He was dressed in something resembling appropriate clothing: jeans, a heavy sweater, and a mackintosh to keep the elements off him. A messenger bag was slung over his shoulder with flashlights and various weaponry both mystical and mundane, and a thermos of tea. Woe betide anyone who undertook such an enterprise without a thermos of tea.

Despite the early hour, David couldn't help but smile when he saw Dallan behind the wheel, and he scrambled into the passenger seat to buckle in. "Did you sleep well?" he asked, immediately hating that he went with the banal first.

"Eventually." Dallan smiled a knowing little smile that went over David's head but still made him feel a bit flustered. "I see you're well-kitted out for this. Good job."

"I'm not entirely hopeless, just mostly." David took the ribbing good-naturedly, and Dallan headed back out toward the crime scene. "Whom do you suppose we'll find out there in the woods at dawn? I've never met a sprite or elemental."

"Well, they're not demonic or angelic, so it'll not do thinking of them in those terms. They're neither good nor bad, they simply are. They are as different in form as you can possibly imagine, from immense sentient trees to wee flitting beasties the size of dragonflies." Dallan drove fast, but there was an underlying competence to it that made David melt into his seat rather than feel anxious like he should.

"So they're completely alien? I've never met anything or anyone who was just...morally neutral." To David, that sounded impossible.

"Maybe you just haven't realised it yet. I've heard tell there are devils that are completely morally neutral. Everything completely contractual, no malice, no rage or anger. The humans who sign their contracts know what they're signing." Dallan looked over at David thoughtfully.

David's lips tightened. "They're moral in the same way that those payday lenders are moral. The humans who sign contracts promising their souls often do it to save a sick loved one, or to get themselves out of situations that are completely inescapable and intolerable. Those kinds of devils are some of the worst, to my mind."

"And the humans who sell their souls for fame and fortune and self-gain?"

"I've never had cause or willingness to help one of them escape their contract." David could be ruthless when he made judgment calls. "Humans aren't always hapless victims."

"You've actually succeeded in breaking a contract and had the human and you walk away in one piece?" Dallan looked at David, eyes a little wide. It must sound impressive—the sheer will it took to break a demonic contract was no joke.

"Four times. Those devils always have something they want more than that human's soul. Figure out what it is, give it to them, and everyone walks away." Not necessarily happy, but alive.

"Which brings me back to my point about them being neither good nor evil. Predators are neither good nor evil by nature. Of course, there are always predators that need to be put down. The Sluagh feed off the unwholesome dark whisperings of the worst of humankind. I don't decide to put one down because he feeds off a rapist. But when one starts feeding straight from the vein, taking innocents and making those dark whispers live and breathe... It needs to be destroyed. It's gone rabid."

"I think we'll have to agree to disagree about the nature of good and evil." Dallan passed a slow-moving semi, and David thought for certain he managed to magically avoid the oncoming car that he really should have hit but didn't.

David unclenched his fists from the dashboard and door and took a deep breath. "How'd you keep from hitting that car?"

"I can't give out all my secrets, now, can I? Just relax, you're perfectly safe with me." Dallan flashed him a grin and sped on down the highway, accomplishing the drive in half the time it had taken David the day before.

David slowly relaxed back into the seat, wary but willing to believe. "Are there any rules I should be aware of? Etiquette?"

Dallan pulled off onto the side of the road, a safe distance from the rare passing vehicle. "They're a capricious lot. They likely won't ask anything damaging, more whatever they consider to be fun at the moment. Good thing you brought the tea. I assume it has milk and sugar?" At David's nod, he continued. "It'll make a perfect offering, then. C'mon, let's go make our introductions." He grinned, appearing ready to take on the world as usual. If only David were half so confident.

The trek down to the crime scene was still clearly demarcated with yellow tape, so finding it again was easy. Not that David would ever forget, in a million years, but it was nice not to have to think about it too much. When they were standing in the clearing once more, David's gut clenched from the saturation of magic and the lingering stench of death. "It's obscene. To take such a lovely place and defile it."

Dallan regarded him from where he crouched, creating a tiny altar out of sticks and leaves and stones. "You're right. This is the equivalent of desecrating my church."

David cleared his throat and went to look more closely at what Dallan was doing. He took some small, pretty stones from his pockets, and a dried sprig of spring flowers. "Now would be the time for that cup of tea." After it was poured in the aluminum cup, the tea was set in the middle of the altar, with the other offerings around it.

"This is it? Now we hope it worked?" David asked, looking around the clearing.

"Aye, it worked," came a high, mischievous voice from behind David, along with a tap on the shoulder that made him jump. He and Dallan both started and turned to look at the elemental. She was tiny, not topping four feet, and nut brown with a cascade of auburn braids down her back and sides and eyes a shade of green one didn't see outside new spring leaves. "Ye found me."

Naked as the day she was...well, not born, but made... The elemental came to stand in front of them, reaching down to take the cup of tea. "I've not had tea in an age." She stepped back a few paces, as if suddenly wary after the fact, her head cocking to one side. "Ye want summat from me, yes?"

Dallan nodded slowly, keeping his hands visible. David picked up to do the same, showing they were no threat. "We're here about the boy, and what killed him."

"Och, that were a horrible night. Don't know if I'll ever get my home to rights again. But I don't trust the both of ye. Neither human, and down here reeking of magic. Take yer clothes off, and then we can talk."

David's jaw dropped, and he floundered like a landed fish. "Naked? I...I can't, I'm sorry..."

"Then I canna trust ye didn't come here armed, now can I?" The little being fixed him with a hard eye.

"David, I won't look. You have my word. My lady, I'm going to step forward a few paces, and then we'll comply. Is that all right?" Dallan didn't sound particularly surprised.

"I suppose it'll have to be, since I doubt ye'll just up and leave me be." She crossed her arms over her small breasts. "My name is Nynia, by the way, my lord, and don't be putting on false modesty with me."

Dallan flushed a bit, as though he were as exposed as David felt. "Nynia. Pleased to meet you." And with that, Dallan stripped without fuss or show down to skin, baring a body that was broad through the chest and shoulders, corded with well-used muscle and surprisingly few, very old scars. Not that David was looking. Especially, he wasn't looking anywhere below the waist.

"Come on, lad, I'm freezing my bollocks off. I can't see a thing." Dallan's encouragement startled David, and he stripped with the grace of a baby deer trying to walk on ice, all elbows and knees and nearly falling over getting out of his boots. *Please don't let him look. Please don't let her talk about it.*

Nynia's brows rose when she looked at David, and when she did a slow circuit around both of them to ensure they weren't armed, her breath hissed out when she saw his back. That was all the comment she made till she got all the way round the front again. "All right, put yer clothes back on and we can chat civil-like." She perched primly on a log with her tea. "Though I must say, I've never seen two people who wanted to look at each other more than the two of ye."

David was sure his blush threatened fatal levels again, but Dallan just chuckled under his breath. "Nynia, he's just a lad. Go easy on him."

"Yer 'just a lad' got an eyeful of ye, and it's a pity ye canna return the favour." Nynia looked at David narrowly, as if finding him utterly puzzling.

"I...I just... You were in front of me..." David scrambled into his jeans first and then covered his back up again. "I'm sorry, Dallan."

"Don't be." He looked back at the mostly clothed David. "It's not like she's wrong about any of it." That was the closest that he'd come to outright mentioning the attraction roiling between them.

"It's complicated, Dallan, I...I can't..." David fumbled for words to explain the sheer magnitude of "can't," but they wouldn't come.

Nynia cleared her throat. "As amusing as all this is, an' it were plenty amusing, ye want to know about the Sluagh killed the boy last night."

"So it was a Sluagh?" Dallan pulled on his boots, somehow staying enviably steady.

"Ye know Sluagh... The name for one is the same as the name for many. It was many Sluagh. A pack of six. Never saw such a thing." She tsked and sipped her tea.

"More than one? Together? They never hunt together." Dallan shook his head. It couldn't be right.

"They also don't rip little boys apart. Traditionally." Nynia shrugged. "The times are changing, an' don't tell me ye've not felt it, Hunt Master."

Hunt Master? David had to find his own log to sit on. This was all so much, so strange. If she were a demon, he'd be on his proper footing. But she wasn't a demon, and apparently Dallan was not just a man (and if he were honest with himself, he'd have to admit he already knew that). And *neither of you human,* she'd said. At least she could be wrong about one thing. He was all too painfully human.

"Are they nesting in your woods, Nynia?" Dallan asked.

Dallan's worried glance let David know he hadn't missed the minor break with reality he was having on a nearby log.

"Nae, as if I would let them!" she huffed, but it was mostly bravado.

"You would have saved that boy if you'd been able, wouldn't you?" Dallan asked softly, gently.

"If I'd been able." The elemental deflated. "They were too many. One, I could have torn to pieces. The poor wee thing." Many elementals cared little for humans, and perhaps Nynia was among them, but wild things protected their young.

"But you did what you could for him, after." David finally spoke up, his voice as gentle as Dallan's. "You cleaned his face, wove the yarrow into his hair. You even made a circle where we'd be sure to see every detail. Thank you for that."

"Ye were all the talk when ye came here those years ago," Nynia said, tilting her head and looking at David. "Now I see yer not a rude one, not to come declare yerself, so you must be ignorant instead. Ye and that little girl."

"I don't know what you're referring to." David clamped down hard, walls flying up that had been starting to crumble. Call him into question all you want, but leave Rhian out of it.

Dallan winced a little, as if he'd felt the walls slam into place. "About the Sluagh pack. Do you know where they nest?"

"They move this way, they move that way, but they are partial to that marshy area close to the estuary." The small earth elemental slid off the log and very politely returned the cup to the altar. "Ye'll be knowing they're most vulnerable at noontide and full moons. Anytime where light shines on their kind."

Those were her last words, as full dawn broke through the heavy forest, and she dissolved into the particles of light.

David looked at Dallan, shaking his head. "Dallan, you could have warned me."

"I didn't know rightly what to expect myself. They're all different. Nynia was quite the kindhearted one; we were lucky." Dallan finished lacing up his boots and left everything on the altar save the thermos cup.

"Lucky? She stripped us naked, and called me and my child inhuman. Not exactly the most polite reception." And for all of it, David couldn't get the image of Dallan's body out of his mind. His own body sang with the ambient magic, and he wanted to scream or hit or fuck. Preferably fuck.

"Even so." Dallan took up David's messenger bag as he managed to angrily tie his own bootlaces and irritably zip up his mac.

"No point in taking it out on harmless articles of clothing."

"I don't want to take it out on you," David hissed, coiling up onto his feet and clenching his fists at his sides.

"You do. That's the problem." Dallan stepped in, close, and didn't seem surprised to find those two fists now closed into the heavy wool of his sweater. "I'm right here, lad."

David yanked Dallan in and kissed him. Hard. Dallan moved into it, lips parting for the onslaught, his tongue meeting David's and roughly pushing against it. It was more devouring than kissing, and David groaned deep in his chest, hands unclenching to slide around Dallan's neck and bring their bodies together. He had to bend into the kiss, and it gave him the illusion of control. It was only an illusion, though.

Dallan pulled back and whispered, "No," against David's lips.

David froze, and the sound that came out of him was almost a whimper. "Please." If only Dallan knew what it cost him to say that one word.

"I'm not going to let you use this to drive me away." Dallan's voice was rough with his own hunger, as he gripped David's slim hips and squeezed hard, making him whimper louder and buck against the restraint.

"This is the opposite of driving you away," David ground out, mouth still an inch from Dallan's.

"And once it's done, once I've fucked you, I'll be exactly the kind of man you hate. It'll be easy enough to work with me, but the temptation for anything more'll be gone."

And that was how David knew that Dallan saw right through him. David released Dallan and turned his back on him, curling his arms around himself. "You're dangerous, Dallan." David's illusions were all he had.

"Ah, lad..." Dallan laid his hands on David's shoulders, provoking a pained shudder, and pulled him against his chest lightly, leaving him room to move away. "When it comes to you, all I want is everything."

Part Two

Dallan

Chapter Six

The school morning uproar was due to be in full effect when they pulled back up at the Shaughnessy house, and Dallan had to remind himself how little time had really passed. His body still ached with David's touch, and though he knew damned well he'd done the only right thing, he could still regret it.

You've got a terrible bad case of David Shaughnessy. He shook his head and put the SUV in park, finding a smile for the other man. "Are you all right, then?"

David nodded and then cleared his throat after a ride spent in silence. "I owe you an apology for my behaviour. It was deplorable."

"No, David, no apologies needed. We'll need to have a reckoning eventually. You know that, I hope. What's between us is taking a life of its own with every moment we spend together." And Dallan knew there were few enough of those, if their hunt went as well as he hoped it would.

"Oh God, don't call it that. It sounds so grim." David tried to laugh, but it came out strangled.

"A conversation, then. Because I'm not just walking away from you, David. I cannot. I will not." Dallan caught David's eyes and held them, determination steady and will strong.

"Dallan…" David held Dallan's gaze steadily. "I'm scars and nightmares held together with duct tape. We can converse all you like, but that doesn't change the facts."

"Nice try, but I see better than most. I see you, David. We'll have that conversation, and it won't go the way you think." It wouldn't end with Dallan just walking away from whatever horror show David thought he was hiding. "Now, should we help out your sister with breakfast?"

David nodded and ducked out of the SUV, color high in his cheeks again. "It's a madhouse, generally speaking."

The house was actually suspiciously quiet when they went in, and Dallan saw David check his phone. No, the bus hadn't picked up yet. They found everyone in the family room, clustered around Arthur, who was balled up on the sofa, crying. Saoirse was stroking his hair, but she looked up gratefully when David entered, Dallan trailing behind.

"Oh no," David said softly, eyes crinkling at the corner with sympathy. "Saoirse, you want to get everyone else out the door? I'll stay with Arthur." She nodded and herded the others out, including Viva who was lagging and trying so hard to get Dallan's attention she was practically turning herself inside out. He snagged her from the lineup and put her on his hip, and turned back to see what was wrong with the boy.

David knelt down next to Arthur and took off his glasses, setting them aside. It was like a cue for the little boy to launch himself into David's arms, and David held him firmly. "Shh, love... I know, just let it out, sweetheart." The other kids had finished breakfast and were out the door for the bus before he finally calmed.

Dallan wasn't sure he should be watching this, but he felt he had to know this family, these extraordinary people. They felt like home, and he didn't want to leave them. Eventually, the boy cried himself out, and David let him curl back up on the couch, covering him with a crocheted throw. "Can you tell me who it was? And why didn't you say something last night, love?"

"The...the same boys. They just shoved me around a little, into some lockers, but they called me the most awful names and..." The little boy started to hyperventilate again, but David rubbed his back until he calmed down again. "I was just so proud of my grades yesterday, I didn't want to ruin it. I thought...thought I could *not* do this for once."

"Arthur, love, this is not your fault. We couldn't be more proud of you, grades or not. You're our genius superscientist, aren't you?" David bit his lip hard, obviously angry. Dallan was angry, too, just hearing about it. Back in the day, the conventional wisdom was that children like Arthur needed to be "toughened up." He hadn't subscribed to it then, and he didn't now.

Arthur managed a small smile and nodded. "When are you getting me my la-BOR-atory again?"

David laughed softly. "When you figure out where you want your secret lair, I'll find a way, I promise."

Saoirse passed Dallan with a small white pill and a glass of water. "Why don't you take your meds and have a wee rest, love? Then we'll get you to school." And have a hell of a talk with an administrator, Dallan heard going unsaid. Arthur took the pill, and David gathered him up into his arms, carrying him upstairs to his room for a short rest.

Dallan took Viva to the kitchen to finish her breakfast and help Saoirse tidy up. Five minutes later, David was back down, livid. "How many times, Saoirse?"

"Since we adopted him, this year, this month..." She shook her head, curls flying. "Those little bastards."

"Bullies, then?" Dallan felt strange asking, but they both turned to him and nodded as one.

"Arthur isn't just smart, he's a certified genius. He's also the youngest kid in the gifted program at his school, and he's the only black student in the program." David sounded disgusted. "The little bastards won't keep their hands off him, and you can guess what they call him. It's gotten bad enough that he's on anxiety meds as needed, and we're trying to find him a private school with a strong enough curriculum."

"And the school just…lets them?" Dallan furrowed his brow.

"They're smart about it," Saoirse said. "They do it when no one's there to watch. Then it's just twitchy little Arthur Shaughnessy being high-strung." She threw the rag down on the counter she'd been cleaning.

"I'll take him in after he's rested up a bit, and I'll have words with the principal. Again." David sighed, and his sister nodded and retrieved the cloth and folded it.

"They don't want to believe their precious little darlings are so vicious." Dallan could see that his words hit a nerve as David took a deep breath and looked at him.

"Yes, I think that's exactly it. Arthur is an outsider, and there's nothing people hate more. Let's go up and get a little work done before I take him in. Are we going to be out in the marshes at noon?" David headed for the stairs and Dallan followed, trying not to stare at his ass and trying harder not to wish he'd got a look earlier in the glen.

"Aye, we should be." They approached the workroom door, and Dallan found himself fixed in David's ice-blue gaze.

"Give me your hand," he murmured, and Dallan complied. David pressed it on the door in a place that seemed nondescript but tingled under his palm. He repeated a phrase in Enochian, and a brief flare of pain shot up Dallan's arm, like a brand, hot and sudden. It was over almost before it began, and Dallan didn't yelp or jerk away.

"You just gave me access." That was the part of it all that surprised him.

"I did. God help me for being a trusting fool, but I did." David smiled shyly, and Dallan's heart melted just that little bit more.

"Now this is the keyphrase." He repeated it slowly, and Dallan gave it back to him with his hand on the door, which obligingly swung open.

"Again you honour me." Dallan didn't know what to say that wouldn't be too much, especially after the aborted dalliance in the woods that was definitely topic non grata. If only he'd been able to have David right there, but his sweet David's desperation and fear were so strong he could have slashed them with his sword. *Ah, if only I could just cut it all away from him.*

"Yes. Well." David cleared his throat and sat on one end of the sofa. "How do you kill a Sluagh?"

"Same way you kill most any of the Fae—with cold iron." Dallan sat carefully at the far end of the sofa.

"I don't exactly have anything like that lying around, and my sword skills are a little bit nonexistent. So my service pistol won't do a damned thing, then?" David bit his lip and fidgeted with his hands.

"I'm afraid not. I'd tell you to stay here and keep doing research, but why do I know you'd tell me to fuck off?" Dallan practically had to sit on his own hands to keep from gripping David's. He sighed. "Bullets will slow them down, but only that."

"Of course I'd tell you to fuck off. This is my job. And thankfully, I'm a very good shot." David smiled and checked his phone. "I should get Arthur to school, and then there'll be just enough time to head by the station to get the gear we'll need and get back out to the site."

Dallan nodded. "I'll stay right here and do some research of my own on Dark Fae running in packs. Surely this can't be the first time."

David left, and Dallan watched him go, a now-familiar tug in his chest at the sight of him leaving. *Like he's left too many times.* But that was daft; he was only going to drive Arthur to school, not off to war.

Part of Dallan hoped that they didn't find the pack today. The full moon was looming in just a few days, and at night, he could summon the Hunt. Not only that, the full moon's pure, white light would allow him to do something for David that may or may not be a kindness—free him from his shackles.

Who was he to make that decision for David? Only the immortal Master of the Wild Hunt. So he would choose freedom for this man he'd rushed headlong into loving. What a glorious creature David would be. How deadly, how powerful. The grandchild of a god, after all.

Contemplating David, as pleasant as it was, was not his assigned task, so Dallan logged into the Interpol Preternatural Affairs website and started digging through centuries of digitized documents. Other than Red Caps, who were notoriously tribal, there was little mention of Dark Fae coming together except for Court. Occasionally they would team up for war or some other purpose that benefited them all, but there was no mention of Sluagh banding into packs.

He fired off a few emails to colleagues and researchers back at the Bureau to double-check his findings, and he was just hitting send on the last one when David returned, stony-faced.

"Went that well, did it?" Dallan grimaced in sympathy.

"If we could homeschool him, we would, but we couldn't keep up with his intellectual needs." David sat down heavily on the sofa. "Saoirse may have found a small private school—she's going to check it out today—and if she likes it, we'll go back with Arthur."

"I know you don't want to hear the praise, but I really do admire the way you and Saoirse are raising your brood. Not many young people would want to take on one child, much less five, not to mention doing it so well." Dallan sat next to him again, this time closer.

"You're right, I don't want to hear it." His lips quirked with a smile. "But thank you, anyway. I'll tell you someday why it's so important."

Dallan had a feeling it was something to do with their upbringing, and with Rhian. "I look forward to anything you want to tell me." He shifted a little on the couch, wanting to slide in closer to David, but resisting. "I did some research, and I couldn't find word one about Sluagh forming packs. They're probably the most solitary of all the Fae. I've emailed some colleagues, but it'll take a while for them to research."

"Maybe it's religious. A cult. What do the Fae worship?" David must have noticed the shift toward him, but he allowed it.

"Gods! A Sluagh with enough charisma to be a cult leader. That's bloody terrifying." Dallan shook his head. "They mostly worship nature—the changing of the seasons, the phases of the moon. The Old Ways. The Old Gods. Dark Fae, who by the way, aren't generally speaking evil by human standards, are strongest from Samhain to the spring equinox, when days are short and nights are long and dangerous."

"Any chance of them policing their own?" David asked, toeing off his shoes and drawing his legs up under him.

"Possibly, but I wouldn't want to put lives on the line for it. The Dark Fae king has a history of protecting his own, not policing them. But a pack of Sluagh could be a threat to his power." Dallan grabbed a file folder for reference. "They take a new victim on the new and the full moons." And hadn't it been a mad race tracking them?

"Which means that at least theoretically, the boys of Armata are safe for the next week and a half." David took a deep breath. "We can do this. I'll learn whatever I need to, to fight them. It shouldn't come down to just you."

"It won't. Tonight, I'll show you." The Hunt wouldn't be at full power, but that hardly mattered. Even half insubstantial, they made an impressive sight.

David quirked an eyebrow. "All right. Let's get to the station. We'll need waders, and I'll need to pick up a much bigger gun."

Dallan stood and replaced the file, smiling although he was praying on the inside that their search would be fruitless. It was going to be impossible to keep David out of those marshes with nothing but assurances that the Sluagh wouldn't strike again until the full moon. He wouldn't dare take that chance, so they had a lot of slogging around in their immediate future.

Chapter Seven

The process of checking out equipment and arms was thankfully quick, and Dallan and David found themselves stepping awkwardly into waders at half past eleven. At least there wasn't much in the way of heat this time of year, but the marshes were still smelly and bug-laden.

Dallan watched David slather himself with bug spray, demurring when offered the bright green bottle. He didn't need to worry about bug bites, but he just told David, "They don't like me. Guess I'm not sweet like you." It was a daring thing to say in some ways, outright flirtatious. He must be getting brave in his old age.

David had chosen a rifle, and he had a fair bit of extra ammo tucked away in his vest. "I feel like this may as well be a slingshot."

"Don't underestimate yourself. And if we don't find them today, then we keep trying. You do know we have a window until the full moon to catch them before they take someone else?" Dallan climbed into the passenger side of David's SUV.

"You know you're as unwilling to take that chance as I am." David looked at him sideways. "So off we go, whether I'm prepared or not."

It was the answer that Dallan expected, and he smiled in response.

"What?" David furrowed his brow, clearly thinking this was no smiling matter.

"You. You're very brave, you know." Not just about this hunt, but all the ones before. All of his battles were against odds, and yet he'd survived them. It reassured Dallan that he'd survive this one, too.

David rolled his eyes a little and paid attention to the road. Of course he was terrible at accepting compliments. It was one thing among many that Dallan would have to work on. David deserved his compliments and much more.

Once they pulled up at the entrance to the estuary and found a relatively non-soggy place to park, Dallan pulled out an oilcloth-wrapped package from the back of the SUV. He proceeded to unwrap a big, fuck-off sword, and David's eyes grew huge. It was double-edged, heavy, and yet elegant in the right hands. And Dallan's hands were obviously made for it. They fit the grip just so, the leather worn to match the pads of his fingers, the palm of his hand.

Suddenly, he just looked right. He looked like he'd taken off a costume. He felt that way, too, lighter and younger and stronger. Pulling on a scabbard that fit across his broad back, Dallan knew he must look like something out of a story to David. All he could do was hope that he wasn't scaring him too much.

The look he caught, when he met David's eyes, was anything but frightened. Hungry, yes. Lustful, certainly. Not scared. "That...is a very big sword."

"Lighter than it looks," Dallan murmured, smiling again, this time with a feral tinge.

David gathered his dignity around him with an obvious effort, and nodded. "Well, it would almost have to be. Let's get going." If David moved a little stiffly, Dallan was too much of a gentleman to mention it. Not too much of a gentleman to think about it, though.

The path into the estuary, much of it a protected bird refuge, was fairly well marked for those who came to track the yearly pilgrimages of all manner of feathered folk. It was easy enough to penetrate the murky foliage, but a good deal harder to just step off the last boardwalk and into the muck. David hopped carefully off the end of the pier, keeping his rifle above his head just in case. It turned out to be an unnecessary precaution, because the water only rose as high as the tops of his thighs.

Dallan followed, the water going almost waist-high on him. *Bloody giant*, he thought affectionately, letting David lead the way and his senses extend out into the teeming life of the marsh. So much of it, so diverse, a mix of mundane and magical. Unlimbering his sword, he reached out, hoping not to find what they were looking for. Not just yet.

There was no Sluagh taint to the humid air, but there was one creature that needed to be put to rights. "You ever have folk go missing out here?" he asked David.

"From time to time. Amateur birdwatchers, coming out alone mostly. It's treacherous territory," he answered, picking that moment to half fall into a sinkhole, saved only by Dallan shooting out his hand out to stop his fall.

"I don't sense the Sluagh, but there's a nasty marsh widow out here. Likely been taking one every year, maybe every two. Would you like to help me put an end to her?" Dallan grinned at David, a little too enamored by the idea of a hunt.

"Yes, but only if you stop looking so...wolfishly gleeful about it." David allowed Dallan to take the lead, heading deeper into the swamp.

"But I am. This is what I am, what I do. I hunt. Now keep your eyes open and everything else quiet as can be, yes?" His voice dropped down as they aimed for a place that was sheltered by some rather questionable-seeming willow trees. It was impossible to see what was within.

Behind him, he could almost feel the face that David was making. The stench was powerful, and the whole place was downright creepy. It had both their senses screaming. "Get ready," he murmured. "You'll need to be quick with that gun."

"Mmm," replied David, lifting the rifle and sighting along the barrel with one eye, keeping the other on the fen. "What's this thing again?" It definitely seemed to have his guard up.

"A marsh widow looks like a slimy old woman with really, really bad teeth," Dallan murmured, leading David through the fen toward the shadiest spot where the shadows seemed to gather and writhe.

Black streaks jetted across the fetid water toward the darkness, joining it and merging until a womanish shape appeared, seeming to drift on top of the water. Her head hung at a strange angle, and her mouth, barely visible behind hanks of wet, matted hair, opened unreasonably wide. Wider than anyone's mouth properly ought to, at least.

Dallan heard the rifle behind him fire twice and score two solid hits in the creature's center body mass. It was good shooting, but he knew as he rushed forward with his blade that he was blocking any further assistance from David. Slashing downward, he deftly dodged her black claws and got in a solid strike from her collarbone down toward where her heart should be. It was a blow that would have killed anything strictly mortal, and he'd done her grave damage.

She wasn't going to give up without trying her damndest to take Dallan with her. When the creature moved, she *flowed* in a sickly sort of shimmer that was hard to look at and still more difficult to follow. Dallan managed to figure out quickly enough what she was going for; she was trying to distract him by slithering around him and attacking David. David, who was, for the moment, helpless against her wicked claws and vile teeth.

"David, down!" Dallan yelled. David responded gratifyingly quickly, and the marsh widow's claws missed their mark across his chest. She shrieked with high-pitched rage and turned on Dallan again, raking her claws across his chest instead, shredding through layers of cloth and opening four deep wounds.

The pain always seemed far away in the heat of battle, and this was no exception. Dallan saw an opening, and drove the cold iron sword up and into her belly, sawing upward till he met the first gash he'd made. Finally, the creature went down, in eerie silence, eyes strangely reproachful out of the ruin that was her face.

They always seem so surprised it's one of their own doing them in.

The pain came flooding in when the adrenaline surge backed down, but still, Dallan was more worried about David. If the marsh widow had even nicked him with a claw...well, it would bugger his timeline if nothing else.

David was picking himself up out of the water, grimacing but unharmed. When he saw Dallan's chest he went pale. "Dallan! We have to get you to hospital! Those will get infected in no time!" He immediately slogged over and started examining the deep scratches, rifle slung over one shoulder.

The scratches that were already knitting themselves back together. David carefully reached out toward the warm amber light emanating from the wounds and smiled in wonder at Dallan. "What are you?"

"A very old man, sweet one." His touched David's cheek carefully, drawing his gaze up. "I'll show you more tonight, because this kind of thing is better shown than told."

When the scratches were closed and healed to a faint pink, the two men made their way out of the estuary and back to the SUV. Dallan unself-consciously stripped off the waders and his shredded shirt, trading it out for a sweater from his bag. He felt David's eyes on him, and rather than hurrying, he took his time. Let David look his fill if it helped him come to terms with what he was feeling.

"I...I hate being a liability. That's all I am out here in the field, a liability." David's voice was soft. "I don't know the right magic for this."

"I don't think you're a liability." Dallan pulled on the sweater and packed everything back up again, including his sword after a careful cleaning. "And I think you just might be surprised at what you know. We'll talk it through later, yeah? Right now, I could do with a shower like nobody's business, and I bet you could, too."

David nodded, closing the back of the SUV and then leaning heavily against it. "And, if you won't think me a giant toddler, a nap. I didn't sleep last night, and it's been...a day so far."

"Must get your energy back before the horde comes home." Dallan felt like the smile he gave David came all the way up from his toes.

Homeward bound, the trip seemed to lag. Dallan wondered briefly if he should have driven, but then the silence in the car was comfortable—two people, neither of them given to idle chatter, just occupying the same space. It felt good, if Dallan were honest, and he found himself wishing the ride would go on longer, instead of moving faster.

At the Shaughnessy house, they greeted Saoirse, who pronounced them a complete disgrace and sent them upstairs with provisions to set themselves right. David bit his lip and managed to tell Dallan he could use the shower in his room first. It was adorable, but on some level it made Dallan's heart ache; David was so shy, so self-conscious of something so mundane as a shower. What must have happened to his sweet David for him to be wound so tightly?

He had an idea, but he prayed he was wrong.

The thoughts plagued him as he showered, but nothing niggled at him like that kiss. It felt simultaneously like ages ago, and like he could still feel David's lips on his. There was such an unpracticed lust to it, as if for all the world David didn't really know how to kiss. But at the same time, he knew exactly what he'd wanted from Dallan, or what he thought he wanted.

Surrounded by David's scent in the soap and the shampoo, it was almost too hard to resist rudely wanking in his shower. Almost. He manfully turned the spray to cold for the last few seconds and got over his pesky arousal quickly enough. *Oh, who am I kidding, I'll never be over it.*

Once he'd dried off and dressed in clean clothes, Dallan went off to find David in the office, trying not to touch anything important in his filthy state. "There's some lunch. Is it my turn?" Dallan wondered if David had been thinking of him, just a couple of rooms away, wanting him with the same bothersome ache he felt.

"It is. I'll just be here, devouring all the food," he teased, smiling. David smiled back although he was obviously embarrassed, and then he was out of that room like a shot before the ground opened up and swallowed him.

Dallan grabbed a sandwich and a soda and sat back down at the computer. A few of the researchers he'd contacted were starting to reply. No news yet on the Sluagh pack front. Everyone who'd answered seemed as surprised as he was, which was not particularly helpful.

Sighing, he pushed away from the desk as he heard the door open. David padded in barefoot, dressed in jeans and short-sleeved T-shirt over a long-sleeved one. All the clothes were worn and old and lived-in, and Dallan thought he'd never seen the man look more gorgeous.

In the two whole days you've known him. You're a disgrace, Jaeger.

A besotted disgrace. "I thought you were going to have a kip."

"Just going to do it here. This couch is comfortable, and if I fall asleep in bed, I'll just pass out." David smiled wryly and stretched his gangly body onto the sofa, sprawling out with his head in the crook of his arm.

"If you do pass out, I'll wake you up for dinner," Dallan said softly, gathering a throw from the other end of the sofa and laying it over David so his bare feet wouldn't freeze. "Promise."

"Mmm. Thank you." And with that, David was out. Dallan congratulated himself on not ravishing him as well as the fact that David felt comfortable enough around him to sleep. He turned back to the computer and discovered a reply from an old friend who researched Irish Fae lore at Trinity College. Aileen had heard of a pack of Sluagh.

Dallan,

You've landed in it in this time, and make no mistake. The last recorded instance I found of Sluagh traveling in a pack and hunting was from Connaught in the late 1500s. They went preying on a bunch of young locals until the Druidry caught up with them finally. Hm, weren't you off in the Holy Roman Empire hunting those deranged kobolds? Anyway, the Druidry recorded what they knew of the pack. It had a definite leader. He recruited the others with tales of how much better their lives would be if they just took one little step up the food chain.

No one was scared enough of them, you see. Everyone knew a Red Cap would slice you open as soon as look at you, but Sluagh? At best, they'd make you a little damp and uncomfortable. Not exactly a set of superpowers.

If they started acting on all the darkest impulses they fed upon, then they'd be worshipped like gods, you see? Or so their leader promised them. The records get a little fuzzy as to what exactly happened to Surais—that was the leader's name. The

Druidry says that he was removed from power and rendered harmless, but that sounds like some fuckery to me. I'm wondering if you don't have him right there in California.

Be careful, Dallan. Everything I've read says he's a force to be reckoned with. You'll need all your…resources and then some.

Good luck,

Aileen

Surais. That put a name to the problem, sure enough. Dallan dashed off an email thanking her for her help, and sighed softly, not wanting to wake up David. All of his resources and then some? That meant there was no help for it. They'd need David. Intact. Which in turn meant that Dallan was going to have to blow hard past all those barriers the Vatican had put up in his mind, separating him from the truth of what he was. It meant he would have to hurt David.

And that made him sick to his stomach.

As if on cue, David thrashed on the couch, a whimper deep in his chest, the word "No" on his lips. Dallan got up to stand next to him, wondering how in hell to help when he wasn't sure he should touch him. The nightmare had a strong hold, and David flipped onto his back, fighting the covers and breathing like a blown horse.

Dallan knelt by him, just in time for David to shoot up and right into his arms, his thin frame shuddering with every rapid breath and white light seeping through his shirts. Dallan wrapped around him, stroking his back, feeling the heat emanating from under the worn fabric of his shirts. David wrapped both arms convulsively around Dallan's neck, taking breaths when the sobs allowed. "Shh, *minn ástir*, I'm here. It's Dallan, I'm right here. You're safe."

He kept repeating the words until they broke through into David's fevered mind, and slowly, so slowly, he came back to himself, to Dallan, to the present day. "Oh God. I...I'm so sorry..." David's first instinct was to back off, to escape, to retreat and apologize and hide. Dallan let go of his fierce grip, but he didn't let go of David entirely.

He cupped David's face in his big, calloused hands and pressed their foreheads together. "No, no...no apologies. It was a dream, *minn ástir*, just a dream. I'm not going anywhere."

"*Minn ástir*... I don't know what that means," David murmured, muzzy in the half world between the horror of his dream and the warm welcome of Dallan's arms.

"You will," Dallan whispered into one ear, finally easing David back and down onto the couch again.

David blinked a few times, and then looked around the room, and finally at Dallan. "You feel so safe, but I know you're so very dangerous."

"Aye, sweet one. But you'll also be knowing those two things go together sometimes. In me, they go together." Dallan dared to stroke the backs of his fingers over one high cheekbone before withdrawing altogether. *Gods, all I want is take this from him.*

You can, came the soft whisper deeper in his mind. *You can, and you will.*

"There is some good news." Dallan stood up to unplug his laptop and then set it on David's lap so he could read Aileen's email.

"Surais." David blinked blearily at the screen. "I don't know whether to be relieved or worried that he's done this sort of thing before and gotten away with it."

"It's good to know, David. I think, at least. And you know how magic works; the first step to defeating something is naming it properly."

David nodded slowly. "I think that's Magic 101." He managed a quirk of lips that passed as a smile, at least to Dallan's eyes. "I'm going to go shower again." He was soaked with sweat and whatever he'd been dreaming had clearly left him feeling the need to be clean again.

Chapter Eight

After David left to take a second shower, Dallan went downstairs to see if he could make himself useful. Saoirse put him to work on cutting up vegetables for the night's beef stew, and respected his unusual silence until her own curiosity apparently got the better of her. "What happened? Something with himself upstairs?"

Dallan half-smiled ruefully. "You could say that. He had a nightmare."

She made a face and shook her head, sautéing garlic carefully to keep it from burning. "I've seen a few of those, and they're never pretty."

"He about breaks my heart, Saoirse." If he couldn't be honest with her, then whom? "And it's even worse, not being able to help him."

"Don't let him push you away." Clearly this was a serious conversation, so Saoirse put the pot off the heat and turned to him. "He'll try. Hell, he's probably already tried. Just don't let him. The harder he pushes, the more he wants."

"I think I get that bit, actually. Self-destructive, self-defeating...but that kind of behaviour puts a terrible hold on a person." Dallan had never seen anyone who took it to David Shaughnessy levels, but he'd seen it to lesser degrees.

"He just has so much love in him, despite everything, despite everyone. He's a fucking superhero, but he doesn't see it. You see it." She fixed him with a level eye.

"I see it. I see him. And he's amazing." Dallan stopped the automatic motion of his hands and looked at her, more than a little helpless.

Her expression softened and she came over to give him a hug, as easy with it as David was uncomfortable. "So again, I say—don't let him push you away. He's besotted with you." Pulling back, she gave him an encouraging smile. "You have no idea how gobsmacked I was to find him *touching* you the very first time I met you. Touching you!"

"Some things are as inevitable as the tide and the turn of the wheel." Dallan smiled softly. "We're one of those things. I won't give up." And he wouldn't ask Saoirse to give up any of David's secrets either. They were his to tell, or not.

"My ears are burning." David appeared in the kitchen with Viva on his hip, newly awakened from her nap. "Should they be?" The sight of Dallan and Saoirse conspiring apparently didn't worry him too much.

"Aye, ye great lout." Saoirse went over to tickle Viva before putting the pot back on again. "Dallan, you finished the vegetables, why don't you and David take Viva out to play in the garden till the other kids get home?"

Viva was already squirming to get down and go to Dallan, and David just laughed tiredly and let her go. Fighting the pull to Dallan was a worthless pursuit, it would seem. Dallan took her hand. "Why don't you show me your wee garden, then?"

"It's for FAIRIES!" Viva declared, pulling him along with much persistence and little strength.

David followed them and watched from the edge of the porch while Viva showed Dallan her little garden with its flowers and miniature tables and chairs. "I can see why the fairies like it so much here," he told her. "Although I'll tell you a secret."

"TELL ME!" She clapped her little hands.

"If you can get Saoirse to give you a tiny piece of bread, and you put it on the table for them, they'll like it even more." The harmless little Fae who loved gardens and tiny offerings were no threat to the Shaughnessys. Viva ran off to ask for the bread, and was back in a blink, arranging the offering on a little plate.

Dallan sat with David on the porch swing and watched her preparations. "How are you feeling?"

"Better. Just…exhausted and worn a bit thin is all." David took a deep breath and tried on a smile for Dallan, although it barely reached his eyes.

"All you have to do is stay awake for a little while tonight. I have something…extraordinary to show you. And something just as extraordinary to tell you." Dallan wanted to hold David's hand, but David had them clasped in his lap as if to discourage such a thing.

"I…don't know whether to say I'm looking forward to it or not," he murmured in answer, looking over at Dallan from under his lashes. "Extraordinary doesn't always mean good."

"I think you need to stop thinking in such black and white terms. Good, bad… What it is, is a force of nature." And magic beyond the telling.

"Oh, I am well acquainted with the grey." That earned Dallan a tired smile. "Sometimes I think the whole world is naught but gradients of grey."

"No…no, there are still beautiful, brilliant lights in the fog, *minn ástir*. One of them looks an awful lot like you."

David laughed. "I'm no great light."

"So you say. I say otherwise." Dallan pulled the old man card because, well, he could.

"Yes, sir," David teased.

"Indeed." The word came out more as a purr than a statement, and David predictably blushed.

The bus chose that moment to pull up and discharge Arthur and Rhian. Dallan imagined that Oscar had Things To Do after school. David stood and went to give them hugs, and then they came over to tell them about their day.

Rhian regaled them with stories of a social nature—so-and-so had a crush on so-and-so—and it was really quite amazing how much dirt she seemed to effortlessly collect on absolutely everyone at school.

Arthur seemed to have made a recovery, and managed to wear a smile. He didn't have much to report, just a rare peaceful day. That's all it took to make him happy—a day without bullying. That in itself made Dallan want to go smack a few rumps in retaliation.

Oscar showed up right before dinner, off the late bus, beaming. "We're doing a musical! And it's actually *Rent*! The school version, but still!"

Neither of them could resist that grin. "You'll nail this audition," David announced, leaning forward in the swing. "We'll start practicing tonight."

Dallan laughed. "All right, I confess—I've never seen *Rent*, so I'm looking forward to all of this. It's very exciting."

"Does that mean you'll be sticking around for a while?" Oscar asked, waggling his eyebrows at them adorably.

"I don't think that's any of your business," David said primly, while Dallan just winked at Oscar.

Everyone was in high spirits at the dinner table, even David, although he was obviously tired. The atmosphere was familiar to Dallan, and it made him feel at home like few things had since his last holdfast had died out. It was a sobering thought that, save for David, he would outlive every one of the people at this table. He pushed that pernicious truth ruthlessly away and focused on right here, right now.

Later, Dallan sat with David and Oscar as they picked out a

song to practice for auditions, and he learned that Oscar had a lovely voice—strong, with good pitch and full of emotion without being over the top. He would have made a fine bard. Even more enchanting, though, was watching David's agile fingers play over the keys of the small upright piano in the music room.

After everyone was in bed, he looked at David and smiled. "Are you ready for a walk?"

"I'm ready for a bed, but I couldn't possibly sleep without seeing what you've got stashed up your sleeve." David grinned tiredly and pulled on a cardigan for the walk down to the beach.

"I just need to go to the car first. Meet you at the gate?" Dallan ducked out to retrieve his sword. Touching it in moonlight made him shiver every time, a bone-deep ache rising to just *hunt*, to chase and catch and rend. It was frustrating, having to wait for the right night, the right time, but he was accustomed to waiting. Not all needs were instantly rewarded.

No matter how much he wanted them to be.

He met David at the gate, and saw his eyebrows rise fractionally at the sword's presence. "I see it's going to be one of those kinds of revelations, then."

"Only the best for you." Dallan grinned, glad at last that he was coming out to David and showing him his true face. The snort of laughter he got in return was just icing on the cake.

The winding walk down to their small patch of beach was silent, but Dallan had to take a moment to appreciate the beauty of this spot. It was secluded, sheltered, with some rocks to explore and a bit of sand to relax on. There was a fire ring that looked like it was used regularly.

"I'm guessing this is what really sold you on the house?" Dallan smiled up at David.

"It was. It's not much, but it's ours. It's too cold to swim in most of the year, but it reminds me and Saoirse of home." David leaned against a rock, watching Dallan. "Show time?"

"Mmm... First, tell me how much you know about the Wild Hunt." Dallan drew his sword, standing back to turn it with a quick motion of his wrist.

"The Wild Hunt. I know it's a story that's most closely associated with Norse and Celtic mythology, about a pack of spectral warriors that hunts on full moon nights. The stories can be found all over the world, though, in somewhat differing forms." David recited the facts easily. "Where the stories seem to differ is in who gets hunted. Some tales say that they pursue the wicked, but others say anyone outside after dark is fair game."

"We pursue the wicked," Dallan murmured. "And I've led them for more than six centuries."

David blinked, head turning to one side. "You're... That's why Nynia called you Hunt Master."

"Aye. Now, would you like to see? The Hunt will be mostly insubstantial this far from the full moon, but you'll get an idea." Dallan held himself differently already, seemed taller, broader. Not really younger, just more formidable.

"Show me." It was a soft gust over parted lips.

Dallan casually flipped his sword in his grip to point the blade to the sand. He faced the moon, and a phrase in Old Norse rolled out of his throat at a roar that shouldn't have been possible. Three times, the phrase was repeated, and then, as the last resonance of the third roar died, they came.

Across the water, from the direction of the waxing moon, they came, a hunting party of twelve with one riderless horse at the head and hounds baying silently at their sides. All times, all nations, simply the best of the best warriors of a generation. This soon into the moon's cycle, they were still spectral indeed, with enough form for David to tell them apart, but not make out concrete details.

"My friends," Dallan greeted them, going right to the riderless horse and cupping its muzzle, letting it butt him gently forehead to forehead. "I've summoned you here to warn you of a looming battle."

Dallan heard their voices in his head, but there was still not enough energy available to the Hunt to be audible to others. He figured David was smart enough to figure out the conversation from one side, so he continued to speak aloud. To one woman's laughing question about how bad it could be, he gave an answer.

"Bad like a pack of Sluagh hunting together. Taking and killing little boys." That made each of them hiss, their mounts sidestepping and acting up, even under close rein, at their masters' sudden tension. "My other reason for summoning you, my friends, is to introduce you to David Shaughnessy, our new ally."

The voices hummed, some rising to tease and making Dallan smile. "Yes, he is very pretty, thank you, Alexander." David turned deep red.

"Farewell, my friends. We will rise to the Hunt soon." As one, they wheeled and rode off the way they had come, silent as the deepest sea.

"That was..." David was standing entranced, watching until the last impression of the Hunt left his eyes, somewhere out over the water. "Incredible." He wrenched his eyes away to look at Dallan, and there was little doubt, really, that he would always see Dallan as he looked right now.

"As are you, bright one." Dallan reached out slowly to touch David's cheek, the chilled flesh warming to the brief caress.

"Not like that. Like you." David didn't move away. If anything, he subtly, probably subconsciously, leaned into the slow press of fingers.

"No, you're not like me, like us. You're something altogether more rare and precious," Dallan murmured, drawing close and breathing the words into David's ear.

"I'm an abomination." David made sure to articulate the word very carefully, just as it had always been hammered into him by old men in black coats.

"You're a Nephilim." And they could not be the same thing, because his David was the farthest thing from an abomination one could be. His David was holy. "Your father was an angel. You are the grandchild of God."

David went still, so very nearly in his arms. "Then they were right. Every Nephilim born is evil by its nature. Created from the most dire sin." And then, to Dallan's shock, he laughed. "They were right; but I got it all wrong. All wrong." He met Dallan's confused eyes. "When they called me 'abomination' and hurt me, I thought they were doing it because I was gay."

Dallan went dead still as David nearly convulsed with laughter that edged far into the territory of hysteria. "Why would you think that, *minn ástir*? Why would you ever think they were right at all?"

"Because when I was a child, my parish priest was obsessed with that passage, about men lying with men being an abomination. Obsessed. It stuck with me, and then with my stepfather... Oh, God. I was already thinking it by the time they named it." David leaned against the rock face again, out of Dallan's reach. "But it turns out, all that time, they meant I was the unholy product of a sinful union."

Telling David the truth was turning into the lancing of a sore that had grown and festered for twenty-five years and more. Dallan's heart clenched for him, and he wished for nothing more than a chance to take revenge on those old men and their cruel hearts. "I don't believe you're unholy. I believe you're one of the best, one of the purest people I've ever met, and that you should be free from what they did to you."

"What did they do to me? Other than use me however they

wanted, in the field, out of the field, in their beds, on my knees, because 'you can't abuse an abomination.' They made me into used goods. If I wasn't an abomination before they started in, I am now." David shook his head, hysteria warring with sorrow on his lean face.

"No." Dallan surprised himself a little with the force of his rejection. "No, *minn ástir*, my love, you are not used goods. You are not an abomination. You are a thing of beauty and glory, and I can prove that to you."

David stared at him and blinked his eyes, hard, against tears. "How?"

"By setting you free." He gently gathered up the tears at the corners of David's ice-blue eyes with callused fingers. "By destroying their binding."

"And that will make me free, then? Will I fly, Dallan? Will I be fierce?" David laughed softly, pulling his eyes from Dallan's and staring out over the sea.

"They never took your wings, David. They didn't have that much power. All they could do was seal them away. I can cut them free again." It wasn't bragging, and it wasn't an easy bit of spellwork. He just knew his ability, calm and reasoned.

"Oh, it would be worth it, wouldn't it? Worth the pain…" David ran his hands down his sides. "Sometimes, I feel a flutter inside me. A gearing up, a tightening, as though I were poised to do *something*. Some immense thing. It was flying, wasn't it?"

"It was flying." Gods help him, but Dallan wanted to make this remarkable man fly right now, right here. Make him incandescent, transcendent with pleasure and joy.

"And you can make me fly for real?" David asked, voice trembling, as if he knew exactly what Dallan was thinking.

"I will make you fly," Dallan whispered. "I swear it."

David reached out a shaking hand and steadied it over

Dallan's heart. "Oath accepted. At the full moon, you free me, summon the Hunt, and we put an end to this." He withdrew his hand, and after a few deep breaths, he looked at the beach around them. "I think I might love you, too. Isn't that funny?" It was barely a whisper.

"It's funny that I just met you." Dallan followed David's hand and took it between both of his.

"It's funny that I feel like I've known you since before we climbed down out of the bloody trees," David countered, shivering when Dallan turned his hand over, pressed a kiss to the palm, and then to the thin skin of his wrist, just below his scar. "It's funny because I'm so broken."

"It's funny how I don't accept that for a moment." David was not broken, just bent. Just horribly twisted into a knot that would make sailors weep. Just hurting. Just lost. But never broken.

"It's funny how much you love me, then. Because you must."

But I do. I ache with it.

"You must know how dangerous this breaking free is. Rome could come. And probably will. Can't have an honest-to-God abomination unto the Lord just living like a regular person." David laughed flatly.

"Let them come. Or let them try. Between us, they won't get anywhere near this place, near your family."

"Don't look now, but I think Viva may have adopted you when you weren't paying attention." It felt a lot more like "our" family than David's, already.

"Does that bother you?" Dallan was well aware that what he was witnessing was shock; it was the only reason he wasn't kissing David senseless right now. He was not in his right mind.

"No. No, it doesn't. I'm not a jealous man." David smiled. "Never had a reason to be."

"David, sweetheart, I think we should go back up to the house.

Do you mind if I just sleep on the couch in the study tonight? I don't want to leave you alone right now." If he had his way, he'd be sleeping in David's bed, protecting him from himself, if needed.

"I think you must stay. The couch is very comfortable. And in less than a week, you're going to cut my back open." That, in contrast, was not very comfortable at all.

"Oh, love. I think I've thrown you for a bit of a loop." He stopped David at the back door for a kiss on the cheek. "You need to get some proper rest. I'll just be in the study, all right?"

"Yes. I...I'm sorry I'm acting like this. It's not like me at all. I just..." The laughter crept back in around the edges of David's voice. "My whole life's been a lie."

"Not your whole life. Not who you are." Dallan maneuvered them into the house, and steered David toward his room.

"Mmm, that's right. Because you think I'm so pure and all that." David rolled his eyes expressively. "I'm really not, you know. I'm not pure. I'm just damaged."

"There's so much to unpack in that sentence that it kind of makes my head ache. Go to bed, *minn ástir*. Rest."

David went into his room, still shaking his head, and Dallan went on up to the couch in the study, with the waxing moon shining into the room through the windows. David may have passed out when his head hit the pillow, but sleep was a long time coming to Dallan.

Chapter Nine

After that night, Dallan just closed out his account at the hotel and moved his few bags into the Shaughnessy study. He didn't mind the couch, and neither he nor David could resist their gravitational pull toward each other enough to send him off every night. It was all faintly ridiculous, but Dallan saw no need to be separated if they didn't need to be.

On the third night, David gently shook him awake, his mouth set in a grim line. "We have a call-out."

"What? It's not time for them to take another victim." They'd been patrolling that estuary every day at noon to no avail.

"Well, there's another victim," David said, voice clipped. "I'll meet you downstairs. Just let me get dressed, and then we'll see what we're dealing with."

Dallan pulled on jeans and a sweater and his heavy boots, grabbing his mac against the chill in the air. David was dressed in trousers and a white button-down with a jacket, and there was no way he was going to stay warm like that. Dallan handed him his own mac and then took the keys and the address they were going to.

Bundled into the passenger seat, David fiddled with his phone and radiated nervous energy. It was easy to find the right spot—there were already police cruisers and an ambulance blocking off the filthy alley downtown.

They crossed the cordon and found Captain Ishiguro already there, pacing around the small body lying in the harsh glare of the spotlights. The CSI team withdrew from their work so that the detectives could get a fresh view of the atrocity.

A boy of no more than twelve lay gutted. Only this time there'd been no one to bear witness, no one to plait flowers into his hair. While there were ropes of intestines heaved out of the boy's body cavity, the display lacked the sheer theatricality on display in the first killing, the flair to the horror that the Sluagh left in their wake.

Dallan crouched over the body, while the captain stood over them, jaw clenched. "I thought you promised me no more bodies."

"This isn't the same killer," Dallan explained softly. "I know it looks like it, but there are things missing, and I don't think our killer would come into the city so directly." In fact, he was sure of it, but there was no way to tell her how he knew that.

"He's right," David murmured. "It's not the same." But it was incredibly similar. "This child was taken from his bed, wasn't he?"

The captain nodded brusquely, clearly not at all convinced. "From a secure apartment block down by the wharf." So not only taken from bed and not off the street, but from a wealthy part of town.

"It's not...him." David caught himself before saying *them*. "There are enough differences that it may be a copycat—one who only got his description from what was released to the news outlets."

"Wonderful. How do we tell parents to safeguard their children when they can disappear from locked apartments?" Ishiguro looked like she wanted very much to punch the hell out of something.

"David and I will wait for them to transport the body back to the morgue, and then we'll take some time with him before they start the autopsy." Dallan stood up gracefully, and stepped back to allow the crime scene squad back in to finish up their work. "We'll get a preliminary report to you before dawn."

Dallan led David away from the scene, back to the SUV. "You know it wasn't them," David said flatly.

"Couldn't catch a whiff, and their scent would be all over him if it were the pack." Dallan sat there, not starting the car, watching the flurry of activity in the alley. "I do have a theory."

"Then you're doing better than me." David looked paler than usual, and his hands were clenched in his lap.

"What if the pack has found a way to reverse their feeding process? There are so many, and led by someone so powerful, they could conceivably do it."

"You mean push dark desires into people instead of using them for nourishment?" David took a deep breath. "They would have to be very powerful indeed, to make a regular person violate so many social taboos."

"Not a regular person. Say you harbour, deep down, the desire to maim and murder and kill, but you keep control of it. Then along come whispers in your head that eventually set you to making your dreams a brutal reality. The knowing whispers that see the blackness in your soul you try to hide, and tell you it's okay." Dallan looked over at David, who shivered. "They could easily grant him the ability to come in and out of a locked room, for example. It's a minor magic."

"There can't be many people wandering around Armata like that, though, right?" David looked around him at his city. "We have our problems, but we aren't exactly a serial murderer hot spot."

"No, I wouldn't think that there are many. But now that the full moon is close, the Sluagh are growing weaker and looking for new ways to feed. Easier ways. They must get quite the rush from pushing a person into this kind of violence. Their kind of violence." Dallan gripped the steering wheel so hard his knuckles turned white. "I doubt they'll be able to muster up enough juice for that again before we catch up to them."

"I hope to God you're right." David looked out the window as Dallan started the car and headed toward the station. "No one's come forward to identify the first boy." A fact that was obviously preying on his mind.

"If no one does, we'll bury him properly." Dallan reassured him, voice soft. "He won't go into some pauper's grave or just get cremated and left on a shelf."

David nodded, turning to Dallan. "You always know the right thing to say."

"I just know you." Dallan didn't try any of his other magic tricks on the short ride to the station, but they still beat the ambulance back, and then went to wait on the uncomfortable plastic chairs in the morgue.

The small body was wheeled in a few minutes later. This time, at least, they had a name—James Rockwin. His parents reported him missing within minutes of his capture from their building, and they were waiting upstairs even now to identify the body of their child.

It wasn't that the second time alone with the body of a child was easier. Gods forfend, it wasn't. It was, however, better in the sense that Dallan could tell within moments, with one simple tracking spell, that this was not a Sluagh victim. He shook his head and looked over at David, who wasn't green this time or bleeding from his ears.

David was deep in his own head, even when Dallan steered him out of the autopsy room so that James could be prepared for viewing. They went up to the waiting area to find the captain with a couple not out of their mid-thirties, the father holding a toddler girl on his lap. The mother stared out with blank eyes, fingers moving to the crucifix she wore around her neck.

"Captain, can we get Harwood to take the girl upstairs?" David asked softly. A morgue was no place for a living, breathing child. It was no place for a child at all. The captain nodded and looked grateful to have an errand that took her away from the waiting room. "I'll find him and send him down."

David crouched down in front of them, fearlessly wading into the swamp of grief and painful hope. This wasn't his first time at bat, Dallan could tell. As a priest, David must have dealt with so much grief, so much anguish, and yet he still willingly took it on.

Harwood, a young uniformed officer just out of the academy from the looks of him, turned up a few minutes later and charmed the little girl at once. She took his hand, and he led her off with the promise of coloring books and hot chocolate.

Dallan gave David and the family a respectful distance, hearing only murmurs back and forth, until the coroner came in and asked who was going to do the identification. He was surprised when the mother stood up and the father shrank back, but David didn't seem surprised at all. He went with her into the viewing room, and Dallan and the boy's father both could hear the shriek of pure, enraged, stricken pain when the sheet was pulled back from her son's face. It was all the identification they needed. A few moments later, David came back with his arm draped around her shaking shoulders, guiding her back to her husband, who seemed to be in shock.

"Is there anyone we can call for you and your daughter?" David rightly focused them on their living child, and did it with a smooth finesse that wasn't at all obvious.

"My...my sister..." The father managed to get the words out, and then he fumbled with his cell, pulling up the number. David took it from him and made the call, delivering the bad news and asking if she could mobilize the family to come and fetch the Rockwins home and watch over them.

"She'll be here in a few minutes, Mr. Rockwin." David handed the phone back, and then sat with them. Dallan did the only thing he could think to do, which was stand a useless watch.

It was nearing dawn when the sister showed up and bustled all three of them home. David looked at Dallan and slumped back in his chair, arms and legs spilling over the sides. "We have a report to give. What's it gonna say?"

"That it's not the same murderer. What else can it say?" Dallan sat next to him, and then dared to reach over and take his cold hand. "We can reassure the captain that we're close to a resolution. I'll make sure my Interpol contacts inform her that they're sending in specialist forces to deal with the perpetrator."

David nodded slowly and stared down at Dallan's hand around his. "It's as close to the truth as we can get."

They stood, and Dallan somewhat reluctantly released David's hand. "Time to face the music," David murmured.

"You do know we couldn't have prevented this, yes? We couldn't have predicted it." Dallan called the elevator and studied David's weary face.

"Intellectually, yes. Of course I know that. Emotionally? Not so much. Isn't that usually the way of things?" David leaned heavily against the back panel of the elevator.

"It is." Dallan was having a dose of it himself. Good old-fashioned guilt. "I keep thinking I should have known, but...how? We've been out in the estuary every single day looking at high noon, and all we have to show for it is one dead marsh widow."

"The Hunt, though... When the Hunt is at full power, you'll be able to find the pack, right?"

"We'll find them. We'll find them, and they won't ever hurt anyone else again. And you'll be there fighting alongside us." Dallan gave him a small tired smile.

"So you think when you..." The elevator opened onto the

bullpen, half full even at this early hour. "I suppose we should talk about this later."

They went into Ishiguro's office and closed the door, and David let Dallan lead. The captain just fixed them with a stony look that brooked no nonsense. "Ma'am, we have no doubt that this was not the same killer."

"Tell me why you think that." She pushed her chair back from her desk a little and stood up, small in stature but radiating authority.

David answered. "Typically, serial killers become more violent and unhinged as they continue their killing streaks, not less. James was brutally murdered, but he wasn't used sexually by his killer. The boy's clothes were undisturbed, the cuts administered through them." David swallowed. "And then there's the matter of location."

"We're currently investigating several recluses who live out in the woods," Dallan picked back up. "We feel we're very close to finding the first killer. Moving from the deep forest to the middle of the city is just too big a change in habit."

"So you think it's some kind of copycat?" Ishiguro paced to the front of her desk and rested her hip against it. "The killer did only follow what we put in the press. The details that we left out of the reports were missing."

"That's our thinking, Captain." Dallan knew David hated lying, but at least this was the closest thing to the truth they could tell her.

"Right. Right. I agree with your assessment." Ishiguro nodded brusquely. "I expect you to wrap up your investigation successfully, and soon. We'll take over the copycat here, Shaughnessy. You stay with Jaeger and find our man."

"Yes, ma'am."

Inwardly, Dallan heaved a sigh of relief. The captain could

have reassigned him, and then what would he do? He didn't want to think about leaving when this was over, much less before.

"We'll get him, ma'am. I know that," Dallan reassured her, and then they took their leave.

Two exhausted, wrung-out men came through the front door of the Shaughnessy house just in time for the first wave of the pre-school scramble.

Saoirse gave them each a cup of strong tea, and they helped with the kids mechanically until they were all off on their buses. It wasn't strange to Dallan how easily he slotted into their lives, or how natural it was to scramble eggs and make toast for a small army. Maybe the not-strangeness was the strangest thing of all.

When the hurricane passed, David and Dallan went upstairs and fell over asleep, Dallan on the couch, David in his bed. Dallan barely had time to wish he were there with David before drifting off. A scant three hours later, David was waking him with yet another cup of tea, crouching down next to him.

"Almost time to go hunting," he murmured.

Dallan took the mug and sat up, careful not to spill. "Mmm, that's right." He fixed David with a look over the top of his tea. "You do know we aren't going to find them like this, yes?"

David sat down on the end of the sofa. "I...I know that. But I can't sit here at home, either. If there's the most miniscule chance..."

"Then we have to take it. I understand." Dallan didn't say what he was really thinking—namely that finding the Sluagh right now, in midday, without the Hunt, and with David still trapped in that human suit, would be disastrous. Not only would they surely die, the Sluagh would run and go unpunished.

It must have been written on his face despite his intentions, because David took one look and slumped back against the sofa. "That bad, eh?"

"Only if you call us ending up dead and them ending up free a bad thing." Dallan quirked the corner of his mouth. "I'm sorry to break it to you, lad, but without the Hunt and without your wings, we're just two lone men against six Sluagh. Six incredibly powerful Sluagh. I'm sorry, lad. I know you want to go in there and clear them out. But that's just not how it would go."

"Would you have just kept going with me, knowing all this?" David raised an eyebrow.

"I...am almost completely certain we would never find them." Dallan knew when he was thoroughly caught.

"So you were humouring me, all this time? And you were going to keep humouring me?" David didn't sound angry, but rather darkly amused. Dallan took it as a good sign.

"It's not so much humouring you as letting you have a direction. Something concrete to do when everything else is in chaos." Which was, ultimately, just what David said it was, he realized guiltily. "Ach, I'm sorry, David."

David shrugged. "We got the marsh widow, so I'd say we still came out on top." David took pity on Dallan and leaned toward him. "Just don't do it again, yeah? Either I'm your partner or I'm not." The word "partner" was emphasized, and he'd clearly intended it to be.

"You are. Always, if I have my way about it." Dallan smiled and took David's hand again, since it'd gone so well last time. Never one to carry a grudge, his David. "Now, what to do with our afternoon?" He stroked his thumb gently across David's knuckles, and his smile turned knowing. Not that he believed for a second that anything was about to happen, but it didn't hurt to give David an option.

With typical bloody awful timing, his laptop chimed with an incoming email. He sighed dramatically and let David's hand go to check it out. "Holy shite."

David got up to look over his shoulder. "What?"

It was an email from someone called Padraig Reilly.

"This member of the Druidry knows some things about Surais. Turns out his mentor's mentor was directly involved in the first incident. He wants to...Skype?"

David's lips quirked, and he reached close around Dallan to browse through the installed programs on his computer. "You have it. Interpol IT must have put it on when they provisioned your laptop."

A few more clicks and the screen was filled with a man who looked like he was just nearing middle age, round-faced and red-haired. Dallan managed not to look surprised or ask stupid questions like "Is this live?" but it was a near thing. "Padraig?"

"Yes, Dallan. And who's with you?" Padraig eyed David suspiciously.

"This is my partner and colleague, David Shaughnessy." David waved once and pulled up a chair next to Dallan's. "Whatever you say to me, you can say to him."

"Good, because this can't wait. I'm sure you're going after him in two days, yes? At the full moon?" Obviously this Padraig fellow knew exactly who Dallan was.

"Yes...exactly so. And you know something about our adversary, you said." Dallan fixed Padraig with a look that said "get on with it."

"Right. I do. I've gone longer than I care to think hoping that Surais would never rear his ugly head again. As you know by this point, the Druidry made it sound like he was killed, but also left enough wiggle room in the way they phrased it to let the truth in." Padraig looked a touch guilty at this; honesty was a core Druidic value, and his ancestors had played a bit fast and loose with it.

"That he managed to escape," Dallan supplied.

"That he managed to escape. Yes. The most important thing

to know about Surais is that he is the most dangerous kind of madman—one with a grievance no one else takes seriously. He believes he should be king of the Unseelie Court, he believes he's the most powerful and godly Fae in the world, he believes he's due undying respect... You get the picture."

"Oh, I've met the sort." And they were indeed dangerous. Beings who believed the world entitled them to certain things simply because of who they thought they were.

"Then it may surprise you to know," Padraig continued, building up a head of steam, "that he's not exactly wrong. He is one of the most powerful Fae alive today. When he makes his kills, he gains extraordinary amounts of power, and because he is inherently selfish, he drains power from his followers' feeds as well. Last time around, they feared him as much as they respected him. More."

"So you're saying, basically, that we should believe the hype. We won't go underestimating him," David replied, resting his hand on Dallan's shoulder.

"This is good information, Padraig. How'd you hear that we were interested?" Dallan smiled at the man on the screen.

"A friend of a friend who's a friend of Aileen. I'm just glad I heard before it was too late to warn you." Padraig smiled back, lashes fluttering a bit, and David tightened his hand minutely on Dallan's shoulder.

"Right, that would have been bad. I'll let you know how it goes." Dallan's smile expanded to a grin that Padraig doubtless thought was for him.

"Oh, please do. Reach out anytime, Dallan." The picture went black, and Dallan closed the laptop before looking back at David.

"Problem, love?" He would lay odds that David was jealous.

"What? No. No, I just... Do you think we can trust him? I'm not sure we can trust him." David pulled his hand away suddenly and crossed his arms in front of his chest.

"Mmm, Padraig? Yeah, we can trust him. Aileen runs a close-knit network, and he said the right things to prove he was who he said he was. What's really bothering you?"

"Nothing. Nothing... If you trust him, I will, too." David paused for a moment, lips pursed. "I just don't know why he had to be so familiar. He'd just met you."

"Oh, you mean the flirting? No harm in it." Dallan was enjoying these mental gymnastics he was witnessing far more than he would admit, particularly the complaints of over-familiarity so soon after meeting each other.

"No, of course there isn't. It's not like you're attached, after all." David looked down at his hands, and he clearly hadn't really connected the dots yet.

"Yes, I am, *minn ástir*." The smile Dallan gave David was intimate, personal, just for the two of them. "I am so hopelessly attached. You have nothing to fret over."

"I wasn't fretting!" Denial, apparently, would continue to work its magic on David.

"Of course not. But just in case you became fretful, you know not to worry."

"I'm not. Worried. Or...jealous." There it was.

"Didn't say you were." Dallan felt a bit smug, but he knew better than to let it show. "Now, what shall we do with our afternoon?"

"I'm sure there's a mountain of paperwork waiting for me. Do you have to do paperwork?" The idea apparently made David smile.

"No, thank all the gods. But there's still plenty of research I can do while you handle the bureaucracy." Dallan stood up and stretched. "But first another cup of tea. Can I bring one up for you?"

By the time Dallan came back up with two steaming mugs of tea, David was already deep into his Byzantine world of forms and filing, the light from the afternoon sun slanting across his face.

Dinner was its typical controlled chaos, and Dallan found himself participating like one of the family. It felt good, right, to be with the Shaughnessys like this. The banter and the good food and the warmth reminded him of communal meals in his Great Hall, only with considerably fewer big, sweaty warrior types.

After sitting and chatting with Saoirse and David once the kids were in bed, Dallan declared defeat and went upstairs to pass out in the study, curling up with a warm blanket and a soft pillow. On the whole, he was feeling optimistic. The Hunt would go well, David would pull through just fine, and he would get to stay.

A soft sound woke him in the early hours, and he found David in the center of the protective circle, moonlight reflecting off the planes of his pale, sweating body. He was dressed in nothing but a thin T-shirt and pajama bottoms, the scars on his arms for once clearly visible.

Dallan wasn't sure his beloved was awake. He wasn't sure he was either, but he still rolled to his feet, pushing aside the blanket, and padded barefoot over to David's curled up body.

"David, love...you're safe. You're here with me." Slowly, carefully, Dallan rested a hand on a sharp shoulder blade, right over one of the wing stumps, which was blazing hot.

"I...I know. I had another nightmare. I just needed to come here. To you." David relaxed his limbs slowly and looked at Dallan with eyes too young to be so shadowed.

"You were wanting me? Not just the circle?" Dallan moved his hand to the side of David's face, cupping the sharp jawline.

"Yes. You." David licked his lips nervously, still jittery from whatever had drawn him in here like a magnet. "You make me feel safe."

That hit Dallan right in the gut, and he stroked along the stubble and the soft skin beneath. "I would do anything to keep you safe, *minn ástir*."

"Means 'my love.' I looked it up." David's lashes were wet with tears when he gazed over at Dallan. "But I knew already." He leaned in and brushed his lips against Dallan's, quivering as though he might take flight at any moment. "I have that feeling. Like my whole being is coiling up for a great leap into the sky." The words were whispered so close that to Dallan they felt like another kiss.

"So fly for me, beloved." Dallan forced himself to wait for David to close the gap again, this time harder, with more insistence. He suspected that David didn't really know what he wanted; he just knew that he wanted, so Dallan gave him an answer.

Mouths opened, questing, heads turned, seeking a perfect angle only to find that they were all perfect angles. David moved in closer, wrapping an arm around Dallan's shoulders as one kiss turned into another and another. Finally, Dallan's lips strayed past David's mouth, across that sharp jawline, to kiss just behind his flushed ear. "So beautiful, you are. Gods." He could scarcely believe this was real, or that his beloved wouldn't just fade away into dreamstuff.

The words made David jerk away as if they were a slap. "No...no, Dallan..." He got all the way to his feet, though his whole body was shaking fit to fly apart. "You can't go thinking you're getting something beautiful when you think of me."

"David, how could I... You are beautiful. Should I lie?" Dallan stood, wanting David back in his arms and knowing comprehensively that he still had a great deal of work to do.

"You're just blind. But when you see me..."

"Who's talking about seeing anything? I'm in no rush." He

wasn't going to toss the man down and ravish him, no matter how much he wanted to. "Whatever you're uncomfortable with, we can talk about as we get to it."

"I shouldn't have come in here. I... I was just being selfish. I'm sorry, Dallan." Before Dallan could blink, David was out of there, leaving him thoroughly, achingly alone.

Chapter Ten

Dallan's place at the table was set as it had been every night, and he was becoming familiar with everyone's likes and dislikes and homework projects and extracurriculars. He and Oscar did the dishes together, David helped Rhian and Arthur with their homework, and Saoirse relaxed with a glass of wine on the porch watching Viva work in her little garden.

The ugliness faded to the merest background radiation when they had come downstairs, and he was swallowed up by this little world of theirs. It felt like home, like when he was still mortal and had a holdfast of his own, full of life and messy and chaotic. It'd become a habit, of late, imagining David in his world, safe and healthy and loved, especially after the brutal reality of the night before and the rawness of David's self-loathing.

He must have been a million miles away, because Oscar had to nudge him and wave a wet plate at him to get his attention. "Saying you'll dry only counts if you, you know, dry." But the boy was grinning a teenager's know-it-all grin. "I'd say penny for your thoughts, but I bet I can guess."

"Cheeky." Dallan grinned though as he took the plate and dried it and then sat it on the shelf. "And also the last thing you need to be worrying about, bright young thing like you."

"Actually, Dallan..." Oscar looked over at him through his fringe of unruly dark hair and worried at the piercing in his lip with his teeth. "It's a gorgeous night." The window right in front of them shone with the light of a gibbous moon, clear and bright.

"Take a bottle of wine, take him down to the beach... Seriously."

"It's not that simple, lad." No one in the house talked down to the kids, and Oscar was clever and too worldly for his sixteen years. "I think you know that."

"I know that you're in love with him, and he's in love with you. And I know that you belong here, with him, and that you're actually good enough for him. You're great for him, in fact. I know he's been hurt, hurt really bad, but you're patient..." Now that he was on a roll, Oscar didn't even take a breath.

"Thank you, lad. Really. It means a great deal to me that I'm accepted here, that you think I'd be good enough for David." Dallan took the next plate that Oscar had washed without realizing, hands moving on their own. "Let me think on it, hm? See how he is later."

"Fair enough. Just...you have to understand. When David found me and brought me here, he looked me in the eyes and told me that there was nothing wrong with me. That I was good, and pure, and exactly as I was formed to be, and that I should never be ashamed. But he doesn't believe that about himself. I know he doesn't. He thinks he's the unworthy one." Oscar's voice had dipped down to a low whisper. "Every time a handsome man smiles at him, he goes cold. Every time someone tries to reach out to him, David pulls into himself. You're the only one, Dallan. The only one. If you don't reach him, I don't think anyone else will. Ever." And that was just too sad a thought to be borne, if Dallan could judge by those big brown eyes.

"Bloody hell, you have a keen eye." Every single person under David and Saoirse's roof was unique in some way. Generally, they were remarkable in ways that virtually ensured they would be hurt by a world that couldn't accept them.

"We love him. That's all." Finally, the dishes were finished, and Oscar dried off his hands. "I hope I didn't upset you, saying those things. I just want him to be happy."

"I know, Oscar. That makes two of us. Now, the homework should be done, and I think the next item on the agenda was helping you practice your song for auditions tomorrow." Oscar nodded and fussed with the dishes, making sure they were all stacked just so, not that anyone in the house cared.

"You'll do great, lad. I've heard you sing, remember? Granted, I don't know a thing about music today, but I do know a lovely voice when I hear it." Oscar flashed him one of those sweet grins and then pecked a kiss on his cheek before scampering off to the living room. Dallan poured himself a glass of wine and leaned against the counter, listening to David playing the piano for Oscar. Thinking. Perhaps strategizing, just a bit.

There were things he knew about his David, things that David didn't know about himself. He'd observed, he'd perceived, like a hunter learning his prey, only David could never, ever be that. Be his prey. But he'd seen the man wake from a nightmare on the office couch, white light fizzing its way through his habitual layers of shirts, outlining the markings on his back, along his spine. David had launched himself into Dallan's arms, breathing hard and sweating through his clothing, clinging to him and shaking, his back white fire under Dallan's soothing, stroking hands.

If this was how he habitually slept, it was no wonder he didn't sleep much. Dallan detested the idea of him waking up from one of these nightmares alone. What did he do? Did he stumble up the stairs to his office, lock the door, and shake in the middle of his circle until it passed? Did he try to scour himself clean in hot water under the shower, or did he quell the burn under icy spray? Dallan did not know, and the not knowing was driving him mad.

Every instinct, every ancient, bone-and-blood-deep corner of his soul was screaming at him whenever David was close. Take, keep, hold, protect, love. No matter what, against all foes. But he was a man, too, albeit a very, very old one, and he was smart, and canny, and he knew that forcing David, even overplaying his hand by one card, could be disastrous.

So, the waiting.

But they were close, so very close to the end of his official time here. The trail was hot, the quarry close, and Dallan felt the feral joy of an imminent Hunt rising up, from balls to belly to arm aching for the weight of his sword. If he did not show that hand soon, he would have to leave because he would have no excuse to stay.

Perhaps Oscar was right. Not about taking out a bottle of wine or anything so overtly romantic—that was sweet, but it would backfire with his skittish David—but perhaps this was a night for going out into the world and making declarations and praying the gods were looking down upon them kindly.

Sometimes, they did, and were both he and David not their devoted children?

Eventually, he went in to join the family bedtime ritual. David and Saoirse took turns reading out loud after everyone was bathed and in jammies. Viva was generally out after one page, slumped over David's shoulder, but Rhian and Arthur would sit and listen, rapt, for whole chapters at a time. In the short time he'd been here, Dallan had heard the end of *The Hobbit* and the beginning of *The Fellowship of the Ring*, and he'd caught oh-so-worldly Oscar listening in most nights.

By the time Rhian and Arthur were tucked in, David looked tired, and Dallan watched him come back down the stairs just a bit too carefully, as though his joints were aching. He met David at the foot of the stairs, leaned up to him and murmured, simply, "Come with me down to the water?"

David stopped still, looking down at Dallan through his lashes. "That sounds like a story, too."

"It is, David. The beginning of one."

His beloved knew that it was not just a request for an evening stroll along the beach, that the words had weight. Fear and longing warred on his face so violently that Dallan's gut clenched in sympathy before David nodded, once.

At the back gate, Dallan reached up to undo the clasp and let David through. The narrowness of the path forced them close together, and he could feel how restless and conflicted David was by the time they reached the shore.

Nothing could keep David's shoes on in the sand, even when it was cold like tonight. He toed them off and padded silently to the water's edge, staring out over the waves like he was expecting something: a storm, a selkie, a man walking over the surface, some kind of miracle or magic. Something to save him.

What he had was Dallan, who made sure that David heard him approach, felt his solid heat at his back before wrapping a strong arm around slender shoulders. "Please tell me you're not afraid of me," Dallan whispered.

"I'm fucking terrified of you." And yet David moved in, leaned into the warmth of Dallan's body.

"And yet."

"And yet." Here they were. David turned his face to Dallan, eyes too bright. The pure silver light of the moon suited him, resonated with him. "Dallan, you're wrong about me. You say such sweet things, but you're wrong. And when you see, when you know, you'll look at me as if at a monster, and that fucking terrifies me."

"No." Dallan's arm tightened fractionally before he removed it, using both hands to cup David's face. "David. No. I have seen monsters and monsters, and you are not one of them."

"I am not RIGHT." A lifetime of abuse and pain and self-flagellation condensed to four words. The four words that had been drummed into his head, that had been steeped into his pores, that had become his eternal internal soundtrack. It was not a wail; it was not a whimper. It was a simple, hard statement.

"I care not for right. I care not for whatever vision you have in your head of what right looks like. Perhaps you will never be that man in your mind's eye. Perhaps you were never meant to be. David, my heart, perhaps that man is a lie. Perhaps you are just, exactly, as I see you. Perhaps you are already perfect." He stroked his thumbs oh-so-gently over the sharpness of cheekbone and the delicate, bruised-looking skin under luminous blue eyes.

They caught the tears that spilled unbidden and carefully held him in place when he sought escape from the words. "Dallan, no. No. I am so corrupted. I am filthy. I am nothing."

"Do you think, somehow, that I do not see you, my beloved? Do you think that I fail to perceive what is right in front of me? Do you think me such a poor hunter?" Dallan pressed his forehead to David's, willing him to see the singular creature he saw. "I wish I could gut the bastards who put that in your head. Who put their hands on you."

"Then you know. You know that I am...you know." The words tumbled out as a choked whisper, as though it was David's worst fear made real, that he was walking around with "victim" written on his forehead.

"David. I don't 'know.' I feel." The pain rolled off David in great, heavy sheets at times, assaulting Dallan like a storm so strong the rain was blowing full sideways. He didn't know the details, of course, but he'd felt that very particular pain, tasted it sweet-rotten on his tongue—shame and horror and loss.

"All this time."

"All this time. And yet here I am, like a doddering idiot, standing on the beach and begging you to let me love you." He was. David had to see that. He was begging the man to just let him in, to let him prove himself.

"Let me go," David murmured and Dallan did, immediately, having learned his lesson that first morning in the cafe. David stepped two big paces backward and stripped off his shirts, short-sleeved tee first and long-sleeved tee second, shaking with cold and fear, but meeting Dallan's eyes defiantly. "Look."

Dallan thought his heart would stop. The scars were terrible, and on David's almost translucent skin they were either livid or silver in the moonlight. There were burns, and two distinguishable bites, one from a human on his shoulder, another from something much bigger spanning halfway across his flat belly. A few smaller, less obvious knife scars paled in comparison to the ugly, corded vertical scars on his forearms.

Oh, he'd come so close to losing David. That was a horrifying thought.

What wasn't horrifying was the body in front of him. "You're a survivor. You survived, and you are the most exquisite thing I've ever seen, and I love you so dearly I fear my soul will crack open and bleed out onto the sand if you don't love me, too."

"Loving you was never the hard part," David whispered, eyes dropping, arms crossing his bare chest. "I've loved you forever."

"I should have found you sooner." So he could have gutted every last one of them.

"Find me now?"

Dallan didn't need to be asked twice. He knew how brave those three words were, how much braver than saying "I love you." He crossed to David, wrapping one hand around the slender waist. "Keep your eyes open, love," he murmured, and then he kissed David.

David's heart thudded so hard that Dallan could feel it, and his wind-chapped lips were sweet. For a moment it was almost chaste, Dallan so undone that he'd forgotten centuries of knowing what to do. He was so caught up that it was almost shocking when David's lips parted, and his tongue touched Dallan's mouth and then, then he remembered.

David's eyes were wide and startlingly blue this close, and Dallan was lost. The seemingly fragile body in his arms still shook, and he enfolded David, holding him close to his chest and kissing him as if it were the only thing that mattered in this or any other world.

"You taste so *good*," David breathed against his lips, and it made Dallan joyful and sad at once. Being Dallan, he clung to the sweetness of the words, and smiled.

"This is good. This is perfect." Dallan kissed him again, glorying at the way David just opened right up for him this time, eager and starved.

David's eyes slid closed, and what he saw behind them must have pleased him because he whimpered and his hips pressed closer to Dallan's, restless and seeking. When he did pull away, it was to breathe, but then he shook his head and put some space between them again. "There's something else."

"David, you don't have to do this, beloved. You don't have to catalogue everything you think is shameful about yourself to try and make me stop loving you and wanting you." Dallan understood the impulse to show him, to just say *there* and get it done, like ripping off a bandage, but none of it was going to make him leave.

"But Dallan…" David turned in the bright moonlight and showed him his back. "You should see what you have to work with tomorrow night."

There were more scars, naturally, but that wasn't what drew the eye. The eye, the hands, the supernatural senses of his kind. The white light and the heat came from the elaborate tattooing on David's back. There were black and blue patterns tracing precise, almost stunning lines along each side of his spine, splitting off over both shoulder blades to surround scar tissue that angled in two tilted slashes, fitted along his musculature. These were still red; they looked almost brand-new but they couldn't be, and gods above, they looked like they would be agony.

"Oh, love...who did this to you?" Dallan's voice was so soft, and he reached out a hand, tracing the backs of his fingers gently over the script. He knew the answer already, but it was the when of it that had him perplexed. David was still so young to have suffered so much.

"When I was thirteen and Saoirse was twelve, we were finally taken away from my stepfather and placed in care. We went straight to a Catholic orphanage; apparently our parish priest saw something in me he thought they could use." David sounded relieved, and Dallan imagined that it must be freeing in its own way to say these things at last to someone, anyone.

All of those people, looking at this child and seeing nothing more in him than what they can use. It made Dallan's stomach churn. After a shivery moment stroking the marks, Dallan took David back into his arms, and David leaned back against him, head lying on his shoulder. It was humbling, to be so trusted. "Tell me."

"I'd already learned Latin, French, and German in school, so they put me towards Greek and Hebrew. Italian and Arabic were later. In the first month, Saoirse and I thought we'd escaped at last, that we were safe in our new world. But my mentor had set a trap. He made sure I felt secure, knew that my sister was, as well. Then one night I was taken from my bed in the dormitory to a basement room, full of what I know now were a variety of wards and banishments.

"There were men there, seven of them, my mentor and six others from the Vatican. They told me that I was defective, an abomination, but that I could still be of unique use to the Church. Did I want to go to Hell for the sin of my birth, or did I want to save souls? Did I want my sister to be safe?" His voice was so flat that it scared Dallan, but somehow it would be worse if he'd told the events that transpired as if it were a story.

"And you did what you needed to, to keep her safe."

"I did whatever I had to. Her father had struck her frequently, but he wasn't interested in her body. I knew that here, with so many men, there would be someone who was. That night, they stripped me, laid me face down on a table. They did things to me. They kept saying that you can't sin against an abomination.

"Finally, they cut into my shoulders with a blade that burned, oh, it burned, Dallan. The runes up my spine had hurt, but that was... It's still the worst pain I've ever felt. It felt like they reached in and pulled out half my soul and flayed it through my ribs, like the Vikings used to do."

Dallan had to bite his lip hard to keep his mouth shut. All he wanted at that moment was seven old men's heads lying on the sand before his beloved.

"I lost almost a week after that. They wouldn't let Saoirse see me. I lay on my belly in a small room, and they came in to ensure the wounds weren't getting infected, and to begin my instruction. They left books of spells, of exorcisms. Bestiaries of demons and devils. I had a fever. The whole week and much of the ones after felt like an interminable nightmare."

"They were trying to take your wings. And failing."

David shook his head and leaned back against Dallan's chest. "Don't tell me tonight. Just tell me that you still love me." David took one of Dallan's hands and spread it over his chest, and laid the other one low on his belly.

"Oh gods. Gods, David. Yes. I love you. Still and always." Now, Dallan let his voice choke with the emotion that he'd kept in check earlier. "I would bind myself to you for eternity, until the sun burns out and the moon falls from the sky. I would be yours for all time, if you would have me."

David turned in his arms and looked at him with eyes wide. "Dallan, did you just propose to me?"

Well, he hadn't meant to, not this soon. Not so fast that he would scare off David. If a bottle of wine was too romantic, what was a proposal of marriage? But the words were out, and he couldn't regret them. In fact, he sank down to his knees and took David's hands. "Yes, I did. Marry me, David."

David's head tilted to one side in apparent confusion, as if an already-mad world had just grown yet more unpredictable and dangerous and beautiful. "Why would you want that?"

"Anything less is beneath you, and I want to be worthy." Dallan was very well aware that "yes" was not the foregone answer. This wasn't some expected proposal after a lengthy courtship, although it felt like he'd loved David for all the years of his life.

"You want to be worthy of me?" That was clearly incomprehensible. He may as well have been speaking Sanskrit, although he suspected David would have understood it perfectly well.

David pulled his hands from Dallan's, and wrenched open his belt, stepping out of his jeans and boxers and shivering naked in the moonlight.

Dallan got to his feet slowly, afraid of startling this rare and precious beast, unsure what was wanted of him. "That is all I want."

"You want this." David's voice was flat and dead. Dallan could see it happening, like a crash too far off to prevent and too fast to look away. "Fuck me." It was like that morning in the forest all over again, but worse. So much worse.

Those two words didn't have to be ugly. They could be an

undone, heated murmur between lovers. They could be moaned, ground out with words like "harder" and "deeper." But coming from David, they were a challenge. The only way he understood love to work. He understood what it was to be desired, to have his uses.

"Ah, David." He'd moved too fast, said too much, overloaded David's fragile circuitry. "My sweet love. No." Fucking David like this would be a deep betrayal of trust. What he could do was shrug out of his jacket, step forward, and wrap it around David's shoulders. "Let me tell you what I do want."

The kindness was what finally broke him, the way so much cruelty had not. His arms wrapped tightly around Dallan, and he buried his face in Dallan's neck. He heaved in a breath, shuddered, and gripped Dallan. "What do you want?"

"I want to sleep in your bed tonight, every night. I want to hold you in my arms so if you have a bad dream I'm there. I want to kiss you to sleep. I want you to say 'yes.'" He held David as though he would never let him go, the thrash of his beloved's internal struggle as merciless and pitiless as the tide that was slowly eating away their beach.

"Say yes." It was a rough whisper, as though David were scolding himself, schooling himself. "Yes."

Dallan held him there for a few more moments, silently thanking every god he could think of that he'd pulled this back from the brink. "You're terrible cold, love. Here, let me help." There was sand in David's clothes, but they weren't damp, at least. He shook them out and then dropped to his knees to help the shivering young man back into the boxers and jeans, breath ghosting over the jut of a hipbone just before a brush of lips. It was a distraction, as Dallan zipped and buttoned and buckled. If his mouth was watering to turn just a fraction, to take David deep in his mouth and show him what pleasure was, well...he would wait.

Wise hunters waited.

When David was dressed again, Dallan stood slowly and held out his hand, palm up, fingers opened a little, and he was delighted when David matched it with his own, twining the two hands into one. "You could have had anything from me just now," David whispered.

"Mmm, everything except the thing I crave most, *minn ástir*." My love.

"Our forever." David seemed to be having a hard time getting his voice above a hush, like this was something that could be spoiled by harshness and loud tones.

"Just so. When we do make love, *minn ástir*, it will be incredible."

"What if it's not? What if...what if I can't...without upsetting you?" David bit his lip so hard that Dallan stopped him and kissed it better.

"You won't upset me. You won't disappoint me. You won't shock me. You are a delight that will unfold moment by moment, touch by touch, and you are already perfect." Dallan couldn't resist one more kiss before slowly pulling back. "And make no mistake, you will be transcendent in your pleasure."

When Dallan leaned back, David followed him, pupils wide, seeming hungry for another of those kisses. "Transcendent? So you're saying you're *that* good in bed?" A mischievous light touched his pale eyes.

"Bloody magnificent. Suck an orange through a garden hose," Dallan teased back, sure now, finally, that everything was going to be all right. Especially when David snorted in surprised laughter.

"That's more pornographic than transcendent!"

"Semantics."

Part Three

David

Chapter Eleven

David woke once, early, before he remembered it was a Saturday. There was a moment's confusion at the weight across his waist, and then he remembered. Dallan was there, at his back, and he was safe. He smiled and went back to sleep.

The second time he woke he didn't bother to look at the clock. The sun was slanting through his shutters, and it was still early enough to turn in Dallan's arms and just…look at him. His lips were still tender from the night before, from Dallan kissing him for what had surely been hours.

They were both shirtless, but that was as far as it seemed prudent to go. Last night it had seemed wise, but this morning, David found himself hating his much-lauded prudence rather a lot. If Dallan was attractive to him fully clothed and just moving about his day, then like this—sleep-warm and curled up close—he was exquisite.

Questing fingertips traced the outline of Dallan's pectoral muscles and glanced off a nipple so that keen eyes could watch it contract at the touch. He was so intent on his exploration that he started a bit when Dallan's gruff voice murmured, "Good morning, love."

David smiled up at Dallan a little sheepishly. "Sorry I woke you."

"Nonsense. C'mere." A strong arm gathered David up, within kissing reach, and Dallan's mouth sought his with a drowsy, familiar hunger. It caught deep in David's belly, and it was still a surprise to himself when he found his body moving closer still instead of pulling away.

This time, he broke the kiss and trailed his lips along Dallan's stubbled jaw to his ear. "I like waking up like this," he whispered, making Dallan shiver. "Tell me I can get used to it."

"You'd best be getting used to it," Dallan growled softly, turning and putting David gently on his back so that he could kiss him some more. "You're the one who agreed to marry me, after all."

"I'm also the one with all the hang-ups, or else I'd have you so much closer to me right now," David murmured quietly, looking up into Dallan's eyes.

"I want that. But even more, I want you to be comfortable and safe and at peace with making love." That earned Dallan another kiss, this one longer, and David's legs slid forward to tangle with his lover's.

"I'm not an innocent, Dallan," he whispered, an idea forming in his head and one hand snaking down beneath the covers. "I might not be ready for more, but I don't want you going hungry, either."

"No?" Dallan stroked David's cheek and took a deep, shuddery breath. "You're not doing that thing where you try to make me go too far so you can push me away." It wasn't phrased as a question. They'd come upon that monster last night, again, and finally slain it.

"No, I'm done with that. I just want to make you feel good." Bold words, and they colored his fair cheeks as he reached for the waistband of Dallan's pajama pants.

"Gods. What about you?" Dallan was clearly all set to say no, but David could feel him just there, just beyond the tips of his fingers, aching.

"I want to give this to you. I want it to be pure." No thought to reciprocation, just pleasure for this man who was so lovely and patient and beautiful. "Please. Say yes." This time, the words cost him nothing.

"Yes. I'm yours, love. Do as you please with me." Dallan's morning gruffness deepened as David bit his lower lip and slid his fingers down, under the waistband, to grip thick, hard flesh. Dallan groaned as David made a little sound of frustration and shucked the pants down his ass and out of the way. His hand was back in moments, and now he had room to move.

Room to move, and Dallan was pulling him into a heated kiss as he found a corkscrewing rhythm that showed that, despite his shyness, David had done this before. Just never when he wanted to, to a man he wanted to touch with all of his heart. David kissed down Dallan's neck, and dared a light bite just over the join at the shoulder, gratified at the way it made Dallan's hips ride up into his grip.

David knew that Dallan was not going to last at this rate, although he appreciated that his lover was still holding onto that patience, letting David touch but not touching in return. "Gods, David, you have...gorgeous hands," he managed, keeping his own hands in check.

"And you feel very, very good." David was warm from his ears to his nipples as Dallan stole kisses, and his hand worked down below. He unconsciously pressed himself up against Dallan's hip, shaky with his own need.

Dallan responded by cupping the back of David's head and drawing him in for a kiss far more nakedly hungry and fierce than he'd bestowed so far. David didn't tense at the hand behind his head, and when Dallan arched up his hips and turned himself inside out because of what he was doing, David shuddered and followed suit, making a mess of himself.

"Oh God, God..." David wiped his hand on the sheet, though a big part of him wanted a taste since Dallan smelled so damned good. He buried his face in Dallan's neck. "I didn't mean for that to happen. God, I swear I'm not some out-of-control kid."

"What?" Dallan was a little bleary, and his hand still rested heavily on David's neck. Finally, the warmth and wetness at his side must have alerted him, and it made Dallan smile. "Oh. Oh, I see."

"It's just...embarrassing." And if he could accomplish life from the safe hollow of Dallan's throat, then he would, thank you very much.

"It's just hot as bloody blazes. Gods, I mean you got so turned on from touching me you came in your pants? Do you have any idea what that does to my ego?" The smile turned self-mocking, and he tugged gently at David's chin till their eyes met.

"When you put it that way, I don't feel like such a teenager."

"Good." Dallan shifted till David was the one on his back, and slid his hand over David's chest. "Because you'll come to know soon enough—there's nothing wrong with honest lust. Nothing at all."

"It didn't feel wrong, just like I was making some kind of newbie mistake I should know better than. And then it felt so good that for a few seconds I didn't care." David looked up at Dallan above him, struck again by how right it was to look up at him at this angle, from under warm covers on a cold, bright morning.

"Mistake," Dallan scoffed teasingly, nuzzling at David's mouth. "We should get showered and dressed before the hordes descend looking for one of us."

"They'd better get accustomed to finding you in here." David wasn't going to run from this, or pretend there was something bad or shameful in Dallan sharing his bed. He slid out and kept his back to Dallan. "If you don't mind, I call dibs on first shower."

"Go right on ahead. I'll just be lying here, thinking of you covered in hot water and soap."

Oscar and Saoirse were the only ones who really noticed that Dallan and David came down together a little later, and Oscar was trying his best to make very obvious eye contact with Dallan. Saoirse was grinning knowingly and not caring if her dear brother saw or not.

David started the meal with a deep embarrassment that gradually faded as he realized Dallan was next to him, thigh pressed up against his under the table, and everything was just fine.

Until he started thinking about the night to come.

Later, once breakfast was cleared away, David pulled Dallan up the stairs to the study. "I need to understand what's going to happen tonight."

"What I'm going to do, how the Hunt will work, or all of it?" Dallan sat on the couch and studied David.

"Both, all." The unbearable tension between them had indeed lifted in the fullness of time. Now David was perfectly comfortable stripping off his shirt and turning his back to Dallan. "Show me."

Dallan moved forward, and his callused hands were gentle where they touched. "The first part is an Undoing. At the climax of the spell, I'll need to use my cold iron blade to open up these scars." His voice was soft as he traced the poorly healed slashes over David's shoulder blades.

"All right. That's going to hurt like bloody hell, but it can't possibly hurt worse than having them made to begin with." David shivered a little. It wasn't like psyching oneself up for a root canal, after all. "Then what?"

"You've never had an X-ray of your torso, have you? Or an MRI?" Dallan was stroking his fingers down David's sides.

"No, never. Would they show my wings?" It seemed ridiculous.

"Yes, *minn ástir*, your wings would have shown up. They're bound around your body, tight, like a babe in the womb. That's why I'll have to make two more cuts down each side of your back to let them unfurl. But there is good news." Dallan sounded like he could use a bit of that himself.

"Oh? Because right now I'm wondering how I'm going to be able to fight after all this. Much less fly." David turned to look at Dallan. "What happens next?"

"I reach in and pull them out. And then, my love, you heal. Your whole body will undergo a transformation as you claim your birthright. Those scars will fade or disappear." Dallan looked at him with a weighing glance.

While this sounded like good news, reality was often complicated. David had fought hard for those scars, and he wasn't sure how he felt about losing them all in one fell swoop.

"You mean...I'll really be whole? Clean? Every bad thing burned away to ash?" David's widened his eyes, conflicted.

"I'm afraid it's all or nothing, love. You either become, or you don't."

"Then I'm ready. I'm ready to be shut of the things done to me, and the things I've done to myself." David moved up to sit close to Dallan, close enough to rest his head on his shoulder. "What about the tattoos down my back? What are they holding in check?"

"Well...what do you know of angel blades?" Dallan leaned his head in until it rested atop David's, and then took his hand between both of his.

"Generally flaming. Great gleaming things."

"Mmm. But the handles are made from bone. Your bone. After your transformation, you'll be able to draw your sword from where it's been all along—sheathed in your spine." Dallan smiled and worked an arm around David's shoulders, only for David to sit up straight again.

"You mean I've lived my whole life with a great bloody sword in my back? Will I know how to use it?"

"Oh yes, love. You'll know. You should have had all this when you came of age and your powers manifested. They must have thought themselves so bloody clever, holding your birthright hostage while sending you out to deal with monsters using only their feeble weapons." Dallan's voice hardened.

"And I'll know how to fly..." David's voice was filled with wonder at the thought, the anger at what was held back from him fading as he contemplated the sheer, fierce freedom of it. "What happens to the wings when I'm not using them?" When he had to be just David Shaughnessy, Armata PD?

"After the spell is broken, you'll just be able to...fold your wings away until you need them. No one knows quite where they go. I suspect some kind of pocket dimension, along with the sword. One just big enough to encompass your body in reality, and in the Twist."

"The Twist? What's that?" David considered himself schooled in magic, but that was a new term.

"The Twist is...the magical world that you and I exist in, in our truest forms. In many ways, it's our reality, while the mundane world is just a place to exist. The Twist is how so many mythologies, magical traditions, beliefs, and gods all inhabit the same universe while being equally true." It was unusual to have to actually explain the Twist. Generally, you just experienced it for the first time and understood it intuitively.

"So Nynia lives permanently in the Twist and only visits the mundane occasionally? The same for all the demons I defeated? But you live mostly in the mundane." David was wrapping his head around it.

"Exactly so. My powers wax and wane with the moon, although there are charms and spells and innate abilities that I have in my possession at all times." Dallan pulled David back into his arms. "You'll see tonight. It will make perfect sense when you enter and exit the Twist yourself."

David nodded slowly, curling up his legs to get closer to Dallan. "My head's already spinning, between last night and all this."

"You're not regretting last night, or this morning?" Dallan's voice was tentative.

"No. No, absolutely not. I only regret that I was such an idiot about it all. That I'm still being a bit of an idiot about it." David looked up at Dallan, and then leaned in to kiss him softly.

"Not an idiot, my love. Not that."

David realized it was true. He was a broken man learning his worth, not an idiot. "You say the sweetest things." David was content to curl up right here and just breathe in Dallan's scent, comforting and warm, with his heavy arm around his shoulders.

They couldn't abide being separated when it was time to drop Oscar off at auditions. Dallan was so sure that he would get the part, he insisted that after opening night he was taking them all, even Viva, out on the town.

Oscar bounced off cheerfully, and David grinned after him. "I'm so happy he's auditioning. He really needs the validation that he's as talented as we all think he is...and it's got to be his way of giving his parents the middle finger. Being out on stage, out and loudly singing about it..."

"Ah, I'd wondered how he came to be with you. His parents kicked him out, then?"

It was a familiar but horrible assumption. David nodded, turning the SUV back toward the house. "He was only thirteen. He'd seen those 'It Gets Better' videos and thought that if he were just brave enough, his parents would accept him. They didn't," David said flatly. "I found him on the streets. He'd been there for three months, trying hard to avoid turning tricks to stay alive." Trying hard, but not necessarily succeeding because food costs money. "I had him registered through social services and into our house so fast his head spun."

"It must be really hard for you and Saoirse, knowing that for all you do…"

"There are still countless more in need." David sighed. "It's something we struggle with constantly. But we decided that it comes down to individual attention and love. We'll never take in more children than we can be hands-on with. Otherwise we're just a warehouse, and neither of us wants that."

"No. That sounds terrible. Focusing on what's right in front of you seems to be working. Jen certainly seems to have turned out well, and everyone else is flourishing. Well, except for Arthur and his bullies."

"I'm just worried that one day Rhian will be in the right place at the right time and witness it. She'll kill them." David wasn't entirely joking.

"Nothing wrong with a protective sister," Dallan answered carefully.

"Not exactly kidding around. She can be vicious." For all the inappropriateness of the emotion, it made David weirdly proud.

"You'll need to tell me that story. I need to know if I'm ever to be of any help."

"In time. We have quite a full slate at the moment, so…I'd rather hold off a bit. If that's all right." David looked over at Dallan as he pulled up into the driveway.

"I told you once that I would never force your secrets out of you. I won't start now." He smiled as David visibly relaxed.

"Good, because I'm about to burst out of my skin right now, and I don't know what to do about it." It was still hours and hours until moonrise. It was three hours until they picked up Oscar. Too much time to fret.

"How about we pack up a picnic and take the kids down to the beach? Let Saoirse get some painting done." Dallan entered the gate code and headed in like he belonged, which David couldn't exactly deny. Didn't want to deny.

The suggestion proved popular all around. David and Dallan made sandwiches and packed up juice boxes, and soon they were all down at the beach, bundled up in layers against the chilly weather.

"Isn't it a little cold for a picnic?" Arthur shoved his hands deeper in his jacket.

"Ach, lad, where I come from, this is a balmy spring day," Dallan teased, pouring the boy a cup of tea to keep his hands warm.

"I'm never cold," Rhian added, looking perfectly comfortable in her sweater and jeans.

Viva apparently just didn't care if it was cold. She went right over to the pitted rock face nearest them and stood there, one hand on her hip. "CLIMB!"

David laughed. "I have no idea where she got that."

Dallan laughed too, but he went over and grabbed the back of her shirt and told her to get started then. As she made her slow progress up, foothold by foothold, Dallan didn't let go for a minute, holding her steady with one hand and using the other to point out the next place she could put her hands and feet.

Arthur was looking on somewhat worriedly, but Rhian just primly sipped a juice box and informed him, "It's all right. Dallan has her."

David looked at her and nodded, and then started to unpack the kite they'd brought down. If they were going to deal with wind and bluster, then they may as well get a kite up in the air.

Arthur enjoyed the kite immensely, while Viva kept wanting

to go up the rock again and again. Dallan obliged her, and the two older kids took turns flying the kite. It was shaped like a giant dragon, and it swooped and caromed over the tiny beach like the real thing. Finally, Viva paid attention to it and wanted DOWN so she could go and dance underneath it, as if no dragon would dare to gobble her up.

David found Dallan standing behind him, and he leaned back against him while Arthur supervised the kite for a bit. "You're wonderful with them. Thank you for the idea."

"They're lovely. Every one of them." Dallan snuck his arm snuck around David's waist, and he dropped a soft kiss to the side of his neck.

"So are you." David smiled and turned his head back for a brief peck of a kiss, which got all three kids pointing and grinning and giggling. "You'd best get used to it!" David teased them, taking off to chase them across the beach.

The three hours flew by, and they packed up and reinstalled the kids safely in the house before heading out to pick up Oscar. The sky was darkening, and the time was drawing pretty seriously nigh.

When they didn't see Oscar waiting with the other kids to be picked up, they got out of the SUV and went in to see if he'd been kept behind for some reason. The director looked up in confusion.

"We were just looking for Oscar. Is he still here?" David was starting to get a bad feeling, the kind where his stomach slowly coiled into knots with every breath he took.

"But...you came to get him ten minutes ago, Mr. Shaughnessy. You were even wearing the same clothes." The director put down her clipboard, and worry was on every line of her face.

"Must be a misunderstanding. Thank you, ma'am." Dallan came up with a smooth lie and got David the hell out of there.

"They have him, Dallan. They have Oscar." David felt all the color drain from his face, and his stomach turned to knots with simmering rage.

"They must. Surais must have come the second it started to get dark." Dallan drove back home, using every one of his many tricks to get them there in scarcely more than the blink of an eye.

A thorough search of the house and the beach yielded no Oscar, and Saoirse stopped David's frantic pacing and searching with a hand to his chest. "Where is he? What's happened?"

It never occurred to David or Dallan to lie. They told her in whispered tones, everything, watching her grow paler in turn. "Jesus fucking Christ. The same ones that murdered that boy." She was a strong woman, but also obviously picturing their precious Oscar strung up from a tree. Saoirse sank down on the couch. "You'll find him. You'll bring him home. I don't care what you have to do, David. Dallan. You bring him home."

"We bring him home," David and Dallan agreed at once, their faces set and grim.

Chapter Twelve

Waiting until moonrise was torture. David tried to stay busy protecting his family, and by the time dark fell, they were all ensconced in the circle upstairs with sleeping bags and picnic lunches. He put his head together with Rhian and showed her how to safely open and close a hole in the circle so that they could go to the bathroom, or in case circumstances changed. Dallan raised his eyebrows again at teaching a nine-year-old how to do complex magic in the space of an hour.

Yes, yes, her story. David knew Dallan was dying to ask again, but now was really not the time.

The moon was barely starting to rise when they got to Nynia's grove, only to find her gone, and understandably so. This wasn't her fight, and she wasn't as strong as she liked to pretend she was.

Again, Dallan called the Hunt. The spectral shapes were solid now, under the light of a full moon, and David could make out each of the warriors, from a towering Celtic woman with red hair and a vicious-looking sword to a compactly built but lethal Native American man with a spear and horse bow. They were only twelve, but they encompassed the history of violence within their ranks.

Dallan's warhorse, Sunder, nuzzled at him and pawed the ground, ready to be off as the pack of hounds restlessly moved around his feet, whining at the unclean energy of the place and their Master's concern. His armor slid out of the Twist and encased him in boiled leather and chain mail.

Finally, it was time. "Your shirt, *minn ástir*. In fact, all of it would be best." Dallan afforded no pity, and David asked for none. His mind focused on Oscar and getting him back alive, David stripped to skin without a moment's hesitation, heedless of the eyes on him.

No one had to tell him to kneel. To David, his knees were a very natural place to be.

"Scathach, M'baza, come and hold him down."

The tall redheaded woman and a male warrior from sub-Saharan Africa came to each take a forearm in strong grasps. "We have him, Dallan," Scathach said, her grip in particular bruisingly tight. "Do your work."

Dallan stroked a gentle hand over David's head, and down his slender back. "I'm so sorry, my love. So sorry." His voice broke, but that hand was steady as a rock as he gripped his blade. David felt a flash of blind panic that he stomped down on viciously. Dallan was not those men. It didn't matter if he was safe or not, he would risk anything to get Oscar back. He'd undergo any pain.

And then Dallan started. First came the incantation, in a language so old that David only half understood it. It was a breaking, a rending, a violent spell to counteract a violent spell. The burn started at a cellular level, rewriting over years and years of lies with the blinding, excruciating truth of what he was. It frazzled along his nerves, and took root deep in his belly. David took a great, gasping breath and sucked in the cold night air, hoping futilely that it would soothe the flames.

That wasn't going to happen, didn't have a chance of happening, because when the spell was done, Dallan began to cut. His firm, merciless hand dragged the blade across David's left shoulder, and then his right. The cold iron pierced raw, angry red flesh, and David lost all control and screamed. That cold burned worse than the flames, touching something in him deeper than cells, deeper than biology, deeper than faith.

Hanging limply in Scathach and M'baza's implacable grasp, David shuddered and panted through the cuts down each side, straight lines and deep, from the outer corner of each of his scars. The scent of blood was sharp and bright as the light of the moon.

The pain was never-ending, the tidal draw of it sapping away at his strength, leaving him enervated and shaking, and he was sure he was a pitiful sight. All of the pain before didn't prepare him for Dallan's soft "Shh, love, I'm so sorry," and the sickening feeling of his hands sliding into the cuts, probing beneath the skin for the wings bound to his body with a lifetime's worth of tissue and blood and God only knew what. Dallan gripped each one and eased it out through the slices in David's back.

It wasn't a pretty thing. It was birth. It was messy and agonizing, and everything, from the feeling to the smells, was nauseating. David couldn't think, couldn't process. It should have felt like a violation, this intrusion into his body, his being, but it felt like victory instead. It felt like screaming in the faces of the men who had tried to take his birthright from him with their clumsy spells and clumsier hands.

Long minutes later, two black wings unfurled in the darkness, sticky with residue. The two warriors backed off because he was sitting back on his haunches on his own, fingers bracing him in the earth. David felt that energy inside him, crackling, gathering, and unfamiliar muscles on his shoulder blades flexed, extending his wings with a great *snap* that rained blood droplets all around.

White light crackled along the heavy feathers, leaving them clean and dry and gleaming in the moonlight. The same white light traveled about David's naked body, wiping out scars, resetting his body to the factory settings it should have had to begin with. It was brutal in its way, the light burning away years of pain and suffering to make David whole. To turn him into the truest version of himself.

To make him the grandchild of God.

When it passed, he stood, turning to face Dallan. The magic had gifted him with black armor that wrapped his thin, lithe body in scaly protection, and he stood straight and unbent before the man he loved. He felt more alive, his body sharper, more defined than before.

"Draw your sword, *minn ástir*," Dallan said, voice choking as he gripped his own bloody blade hard.

David reached back, to the cradle between his wings, just over the top of his spine. He felt the knob that wouldn't be there in a human, gripped it, and *pulled*. The skin didn't split and there was no pain, just a delicious shiver as the blade slipped free and filled his hand. Or, rather, it filled his hand and his head and every muscle in his body.

It wasn't just that it was stunning to look at. It was *his*. And he knew how to use it, all the way down every rippled inch of bright steel.

"Oh, David..." Dallan's voice was awed, hushed. Reverent.

"Dallan. I see you now." His strong, handsome beloved was so much more than he seemed. Ancient and powerful, Dallan was full of the kind of strength that didn't require violence. The strength to birth a foal or keep a little girl from falling as she stretched herself to climb. Quiet, deep strength that required no braggadocio or vulgar display. No, you had nothing to fear from Dallan Jaeger—unless he was bearing down on you with twelve angry Hunters.

"It's time to hunt." Dallan was obviously trying to tear his eyes from David.

The clearing juddered with the force of the downdraft as David gathered himself, tensed, and leaped, his great black wings beating the air as he hovered near the tree where they'd found the first boy. "Then saddle up." He felt a spark of dark, grim humor as he watched them do just that.

Within moments, the hounds had caught the scent, and the entire Hunt was off after them. One of the Hunters, a man who looked to be from Mongolia, launched a great eagle into the sky, and it flew alongside David. David, whose new wings cast a moon shadow on the ground as he felt the sky envelop him, hold him, felt the updrafts and downdrafts and minute changes to adjust for as he finally did what came naturally to him.

If Surais and the Sluagh were ever in the estuary, they'd obviously moved inland—deep inland, into the pristine forest where they should not be, and would not be welcomed by the local sprites and spirits.

David didn't have any preternatural sense of sight, so he was relying on the eagle to tell him when to dive. He angled himself in the same downward trajectory and felt himself plummet from the sky. Before this becoming, he'd hated roller coasters and the sickening feeling of falling. But now? Now all he felt was sheer exhilaration at his own skill, at his own prowess, at the way the sky fell beneath him.

David pulled up at the last moment and felt his stomach flip over at what he saw. He'd found Oscar, and as far as he could tell, he'd found the boy alive. Alive, but unconscious, naked, and strung up between two trees with what looked like silver wires. The wires were thin, but they crisscrossed his slight body in thick, knotted ropes that were so taut they were cutting into skin.

Every instinct in him screamed to go and get the boy, to use his sword to sever the wires, to pull Oscar to safety in his arms. It was only Dallan's sharp "NO" from the forest floor that pulled him up short. The Sluagh were not there, and David looked down at Dallan and the Hunt with wild eyes. "No?!"

"He's a trap, love. A trap."

It was only then that David saw the intricacy of the knots, their placement. If he made one wrong move and the wires snapped, Oscar would die pulled apart into pieces. "Oh God."

"Here, David." Dallan threw up a small wickedly sharp knife, and David caught it by the hilt. "Use this, and go slowly. We'll chase the Sluagh."

There was no way to just leave Oscar and come back after their victory; if he woke up and thrashed in his bonds he'd kill himself, torn limb from limb. David held the knife in a death grip, and looked down to meet Dallan's eyes. "Kill them. Kill them all."

"Aye. Kill them all." Dallan barked a command to the hounds, and the eagle was launched again. They caught the scent and were off, their baying muffled by the deepening fog. The Hunt Master wheeled his horse and followed them, despite the lack of a trail or any visible path through the wilderness.

They were gone in a matter of heartbeats, leaving David alone with an impossible task. *Or was it?* Surely, this was a trap on more than one level. The Sluagh knew that whether or not their pursuers tripped the wires and killed Oscar, they'd stop here to save him. The more David looked at the wires, the more he could make out a pattern. That wasn't unusual, given David's training in finding and following patterns in seemingly unrelated events.

What was strange was that, when he narrowed his focus carefully and concentrated, one of the wires glowed faintly. "Useful," he murmured, steadying his wings and hovering motionlessly in front of Oscar. "Wonder what else I can do?"

Next to getting Oscar out, making sure he stayed unconscious was of paramount importance. David switched the knife to his left hand and pressed the first two fingers of his right hand against Oscar's damp, chilled forehead. He matched his breathing to Oscar's and, again, concentrated. *Shhh, sweet boy. Sleep deeply and let me free you.* He felt something in Oscar just *give*, and then he was inside the boy's mind, planting the command to sleep on, no matter what, until he was told to wake up.

It took effort, but David did no more than that. He didn't look to see if Oscar had been violated, or experience how terrified he'd been. No, David had to focus on the job at hand, with the rest coming later.

His hand was steady as he called on all that willpower that had made him such a good exorcist, and he cut the subtly glowing strand. As soon as it gave way, he saw which to cut next, and then next. It was excruciatingly slow work, finding and snipping wire after wire after wire, and soon David was dripping with sweat in the cold night air. He forced himself not to hurry, not to take anything for granted. Each wire had to be considered, followed, before being cut.

Time lost all meaning, but eventually, he cut the very last wire. He'd been supporting Oscar's weight ever since he'd gone through enough layers of wire for him to fall, painfully aware that if his grip loosened, Oscar would lose whatever appendages were still bound. That made it easy for David to catch Oscar and bear him down to the relative safety of the earth beneath them.

"Oh, so very well done." The voice was low, sibilant, but David heard every word, drawing his sword and turning to face its source. A figure stepped out of the gloom, seemingly alone, with muck clinging to his bare feet and the hem of his black robe. In fact, the muck seemed to drip from him, from his hands, his feet, his wicked, sharp claws, and off the end of his nose set in a face that was somehow ill defined and most definitely inhuman. "I was curious how you'd get him down."

"Surais." So that was the trap. He felt foolish, but anger ultimately won out, and he advanced on the Sluagh leader with drawn sword. "I was wondering if you'd dare show yourself."

"Dare?" The creature laughed, and it sounded disgusting, almost prurient. "I dare whatever I wish, and I wish to take you apart, angel." He drew no sword, but he did flex his freakish hands and fingers, claws like blades dripping ichor on the ground and making a clicking sound that reminded David of a host of cockroaches skittering across a linoleum floor.

"I don't fall apart that easily," David growled, half-shocked that he could make that kind of feral noise. He lunged forward with his sword, finding a perfect balance, a center with the blade, and his wings that propelled him with a shocking speed toward the abomination in front of him.

Surais grabbed the blade with his claws, tangling it and then sidestepping, moving like black velvet in the bright moonlight. His counterstrike was swift, and it opened a gash on David's upper arm that didn't heal like it should, the skin slow to knit back together as his body fought the poison. Since it wasn't his sword arm, David ignored it and whirled in place to feel the bite of his sword into Surais' outflung forearm. It should have sheared flesh from bone, but it was almost like the Sluagh's skin was chitinous, hard and brittle. The reverberations passed all the way up David's arm.

"I've heard you fall apart shockingly easily," Surais replied, the words slithering from his black mouth like the poison on his claws. "I've heard that Dallan makes you just fall to pieces."

David hissed in a breath and parried the next strike from those claws handily, moving around to go on the offense. It would be so easy to surrender to the red cloud of rage around the edges of his vision at Dallan's name coming from such a foul beast, but there was Oscar to think of. He couldn't allow himself the luxury of giving in to those juvenile taunts, or the white-hot release of a proper rage. No, he had to block his ears, steady his hand, dig in his heels, and fight.

So fight they did. Every time Surais got a half second to breathe he found another new, vile thing to say about Dallan, about David. About Oscar, for God's sake. Nothing was apparently too vulgar, but David forced himself to ignore it all, pressing his lips together and taking one more deep cut to the pectoral muscle before pinning Surais to a tree with his sword a millimeter from the Sluagh's neck.

"I wouldn't." Surais sounded incredibly calm for a creature about to lose his head, and it made David pause, the hairs at the back of his neck prickling. Keeping his sword pressed to Surais' throat, he looked back to see another Sluagh wrapped around Oscar's unconscious body. Pointed, venomous claws were poised to rip out the boy's throat.

David took a half step back, stomach sinking as he dropped his sword arm to his side. "What do you want?"

"Don't be dense. I want you." Surais grinned an unholy grin, all sharp teeth and foul breath. "Come with me, and we leave your pretty boy for your *lover* to find. He'll be perfectly safe. You, on the other hand..."

"I'll do it," David replied immediately. "I'll do anything you want, just leave Oscar alone." He knew that was exactly what the creature expected, and yet any other answer was unthinkable.

Surais' grin broadened as David sheathed his sword, and the Sluagh pressed his damp, oily forehead to David's. "Shh, now. I suggest you don't fight me."

It took all the willpower in David not to defend himself in any way when the Sluagh's mind reached for his and snuffed out his consciousness.

Chapter Thirteen

David woke slowly, by degrees, taking stock of his environment as best he could without opening his eyes. He was naked, which was somehow no great surprise, and bound spread-eagled on some kind of stone or marble table. It was moldy and slippery beneath him, and the air that pressed thickly against his nose and tongue was foul, spoiled with rot. His wings were gone; he must have put them away by instinct when he'd lost consciousness.

His eyes flew open at the feeling of claw-tips crawling slowly up his bare belly. "Ah yes, I thought you were awake. No more tricks, little angel, and keep those wings tucked away."

The prick of the talons made David's skin crawl, his body yearn to curl in on itself. Surais was not the most dangerous creature he'd ever faced, he reminded himself sternly, but it was hard to be steadfast when he was trapped, naked and on display for a perverted evil Fae. At best he could expect a death like their young John Doe's; at worst...at worst it could take years if Surais had brought him into Faerie. "Where are we?" he managed, forcing his voice not to tremble.

"Oh, I've taken you home. The Hunt can't track me here. They have no authority in Faerie realms. Their magic doesn't work." Surais chuckled throatily and stroked down David's neck with the backs of his claws. "In case you were holding out for rescue."

David pressed his lips together, refusing to answer. Of course he'd hoped for rescue, but even more, he hoped that Dallan would find Oscar before the boy died of exposure. Dallan. *God, I am so sorry, love.* He knew Dallan would understand, and he knew vengeance would come to Surais eventually—there was no prey for him here so deep in the Twist, amongst his own kind. He needed humans to torment.

None of that was getting him out of here alive.

David hissed like an angry cat when Surais stood between his thighs, running his claws firmly up delicate flesh, hard enough to open skin. The smell of blood was a tangy, metallic counterpoint to the sewer smell of Surais' lair. It was all he could do not to writhe away from the creature's slimy grasp as his bleeding thighs were gripped and pulled open so far his hips ached with the strain against the ropes.

This, David could deal with. He knew how to just go away, hide in his mind. Nothing Surais had for him could be worse than what he'd already experienced. The pain was excruciating, claws digging into tender flesh and Surais' cruel laughter cloying in his ears like the sound of rotten fruit dropping from the tree to the earth. David was trying his best to count to one hundred in all the languages he knew, but unbidden, the image of Dallan from earlier in the morning (*God, was it really just be this morning?*) came flooding through his mind. Kind, gentle, strong Dallan writhing helplessly in his grasp, kissing him like he was the only precious thing in the world, looking up at his betrothed in the early morning sunlight.

The pain eventually made David clamp his eyes shut. He would never see Dallan again. Never know what love could be like with him. It was all just too fucking much, and David felt tears squeeze past his closed eyes.

"Aww, that was depressingly easy," Surais cooed, leaning up over David's body to lick at the tear trails. "I thought you'd last longer before breaking."

"You haven't broken me," David spat out, jaws grinding around the words. "You won't break me."

"Everyone breaks. This is just the barest first taste of what awaits you." While Surais was brutish, he was taking some measure of care that he not hurt David too badly, too quickly. He grinned and laughed at David's teeth snapping at him wherever he could reach.

David managed to find enough sass left in his battered body to roll his eyes exaggeratedly at Surais' threat. *All right, fine, I get it. You're a big, bad Fae.* It wasn't that he downplayed the danger; it was just that he'd heard the dialogue before, so many times. Bullies loved to brag about their prowess, be they demons or Sluagh or regular human beings. They might be good at inflicting pain—and the body that they'd found in the woods showed Surais was *very* good at it indeed—but they were lousy at communication.

He was rewarded with a rough slap across the face, and then another, combined with a particularly brutal slice of talons. "You mock me. That is unwise."

"Maybe you'll finish faster and get on with killing me if you get some stimulation," David spat back. "I'm bored."

"You're bored? I guess you're just too used up to be a good plaything." Surais scraped his claws over David's nipples, scratching them roughly before opening up gouges down his flat belly.

David gasped and ground his teeth harder against the scream that was gathering in his throat. Now it seemed obvious what Surais and his followers had used to open the boys up, and all David could see was the macabre image of all those children split open and spooled out like a knitter's snarled ball of yarn by those evil claws. *It won't happen to Oscar. It won't happen to him.* He knew, though, with bowel-clenching certainty, that his fate was to be split open and used to decorate this chamber of horrors.

"Boredom is such a human emotion," Surais continued, turning his face and biting through the flesh of David's calf, lapping at the blood as he spent himself onto the floor. "Ahh. Now that the edge is off, what shall we do next? Oh, I know."

David's head smacked hard against the stone of the table as he fought uselessly against the bonds, setting stars behind his eyes.

"Tsk, no point in fighting, little angel. There's nothing so very special about you. So much suffering you've endured, and you're really rather...dull."

"Fuck you." Sometimes, it hurt too much to get all clever with the banter. What Surais said was worse to David than any of a hundred more lewd and disgusting things he could have dredged up from David's mind. Being insignificant, suffering for nothing, was worse by orders of magnitude than suffering for what could be called a greater cause.

"Hm, we could do that, but I doubt I would be impressed." Surais shrugged and wriggled his claws at David before running them very lightly down his chest and belly, opening ten thin, bright red lines. "Good thing I got to you before your Hunter. You're not entertaining enough for him, but I'm sure he would have hidden it well."

This, of course, was the Sluagh's gift, unholy and cruel—to make their victims believe every dark, self-hating thought in their heads. It worked on David, although a distant voice inside him screamed to remain rational, that Surais was *playing* with him, that Dallan would never, ever be disappointed in him. That voice was drowned by the howling wind of the black abyss David found himself teetering on the edge of.

And when the next deep cut came, and David looked frantically down to see his own small intestine sliding over those foul claws, he fell right into the darkness.

On the whole, the darkness was preferable. He could cower in a corner of his mind and wrap good memories around him—home, hearth, Dallan. It was nothing he hadn't done a hundred times before. The last thing David was expecting in this netherworld was a light.

Dallan?

"No, little one. Your man is still looking for you." That voice, the deep red light enveloping an area of yet more Stygian blackness. "But I found you."

"Ipos." David forced his eyes to focus, was sure he couldn't possibly be awake, and wondered what the fuck Surais was doing to him to produce this particular illusion. "You're not real."

"How rude." The voice got closer, and the red light revealed a magnificent, lion-headed man wearing a graven golden breastplate and cloth-of-gold kilt. He was all shades of light and dark, and he was beautiful. A magnificent demon. "And after our last meeting, no less."

"This...this isn't your realm. This isn't Hell. So...you can't be here." David felt a pang of embarrassment at Ipos's words, at the memory of that last meeting and everything that had happened.

"I am a Duke of Hell. I go where I please, and your mind is well-trod territory indeed, David." In the darkness, David felt Ipos cup his cheek with a calloused hand. "So well-trod, in fact, that I cannot have you giving up and allowing this creature to end your life. You have responsibilities."

David shivered at the contact and pulled away—this wasn't Dallan. Ipos hadn't earned the right to touch him so cavalierly, no matter their former acquaintance. "Do you think I've forgotten? I. Cannot. Move."

Ipos's golden eyes flicked to the side and then to David's again. "Be glad enough you're not seeing what he's doing. Ugh, what a filthy little maggot. Why have you not killed him yet?"

"Because I am strapped down, Ipos."

"Because you don't understand your own power," the demon retorted. "You didn't all those years ago, and you still don't, even after your Hunter set you free."

"What are you talking about?" David's voice was wary, but he didn't pull away again from Ipos, who was crowding him deeper into his corner.

"On a broader level, your truly stunning insecurities. On a more specific level, the fact that you can still summon your wings and fetch your sword. Even now. Even here." Ipos shook his great head, beads of precious stones making soft sounds where they were braided into the fur.

"But I can't feel them." They may as well have been as far away as they were before Dallan freed them from his body.

"Nonsense. You need to stop being afraid and start being angry. I *know* you can do angry. So *full* of righteous anger," Ipos purred, stroking again at David's cheek. David managed not to arch into the touch, but just barely. "It was the purity of your rage that drew me to you, that kept me from killing you in that sordid little room. It was what allowed me to trust you with my most precious possession."

"Rhian is not a possession!" Out of everything, of course David pulled that one part out to examine.

"Expression. Figure of speech. See? Righteous anger." Ipos grinned, showing off a mouthful of fangs that could rip David to shreds in moments.

"Why are you even here? What do you care for me?" Ipos was right; their last encounter had been so sordid that David seriously doubted the demon was here for a repeat performance. But then again, that's what demons liked, wasn't it? Sordid affairs of the flesh.

"Ah, David…I think of you often." Ipos purred, and David had a sudden, jolting sense memory of a broad furred chest at his back, vibrating with that low, steady, thrumming noise. *God, what is wrong with me?* "Besides, I think of her often. She relies on you, loves you. I would not see her bereft of your protection and your care."

"Not when she's still too young to be of use to you."

"Oh, David." Ipos stroked his hand over David's short, sweaty hair. "Is that what you tell yourself? That I leave her with you because I have no use for her? You know that isn't true. I leave her with you so that she can experience the best in her humanity."

"Until you come and take her away." David's voice was ragged, thoughts fragmenting under so much stress.

"Stop fretting over that. You need to get out of this place before you have the luxury of worrying about our girl. Remember what I told you. You're more powerful than you think." Ipos nuzzled at the side of David's face like the giant cat he was. "There's just one downside."

"What's that?" David asked, frozen, those giant fangs perilously close to his throat.

"You're going to have to wake up." The slap was hard when Ipos delivered it, a sharp crack across his cheek.

David woke to excruciating pain and a smell that made his gorge rise. *You're powerful. You have power. Take it.*

Chapter Fourteen

Take the power. That sounded easy enough, but for the simple fact that David couldn't stop screaming long enough to concentrate. Much to his eternal shame, his screams bordered on the hysterical. It was all he could do to hold onto consciousness. That's what happened when a megalomaniacal, sadistic Fae unspooled your intestines like a roll of heavy cable. Somehow, David processed the fact that if he passed out again, he'd be dead. If he just held on a little longer...

Surais hummed while he worked, a tuneless song in a key that made David's ears practically bleed, discordant and soft but agonizing. As horrible as the noise was, David found himself fixating on it, above the horrific sound of himself being slowly robbed of major organs. The dissonance made him angry, somehow, in the midst of all the terror and pain.

The same anger that drove him forward every day.

White heat rose in his chest, ferocious and terrible, fragmented pictures swirling through his mind—his sister, the kids, Dallan—and his back twitched and itched unbearably. He grasped onto that feeling, and held as hard as he could, gathering all his will to focus on the flesh over his shoulder blades and pulling at energy from the Twist, the energy all around him, to just *reach*. He reached so far, so doggedly, like a trapped man grasping for a knife to cut himself free.

With a great rush of displaced air, David's wings burst from his bare back, stretching to fill the stone room. Lambent light sizzled over his skin, healing most of his wounds save the one across his belly. Surais howled with anger at the sight, at the undoing of so much of his very good work. David howled right back, beating his wings in great gusts, their strength snapping through the leather straps that had bound him hand and foot with bruising force.

He was free, albeit with just one little problem. Well, technically two little problems, if one counted Surais, and David couldn't afford not to. Surais was making for a rack of weapons against the far wall, dark light from a spell gathering in one hand.

David took the moment to shove his innards back inside, howling at the pain of the act itself and the searing agony of his body trying so very hard to heal the mess.

The few seconds it took to heal felt like years, but when it was done David felt stronger, crouching on the stone slab and whirling to face Surais. He reached back and gripped his sword, yanking it free. It was noticeably smaller than the last time, better suited to close-quarter fighting. He furled his wings in to keep them out of the way, and leaped off the slab.

Surais faced him with a wicked-looking dagger that dripped black ichor along its curved length, and a snarl that matched it in ugliness. The Sluagh withstood the first onslaught of David's attacks, parrying the glowing blade with ferocious precision. Before David could attack again, Surais lashed out—not with blade or spell, but with the most insidious weapon in his arsenal—with his innate power to strike at a mind and inhabit it, spooling out pain and suffering and taking it in as sustenance. He was *feeding* off David.

David couldn't stop it. It happened too quickly, and Surais was too proficient. Before he realized he was under attack, it was too late to defend himself. He went down hard onto his knees, and the memories rose up, drowning him in pain and the utter, exquisite misery of a life spent largely as someone else's pawn, someone else's toy.

"Poor little Davey, so very young when your mother died."

Pulled from a hospital bed, shrieking, into a nurse's arms, another woman doing the same with his baby sister. The last spark of life faded from the woman's body on the bed, too fast for them to do anything to stop it, and David felt it, in every cell, in every fiber. That sudden, biting, cutting loss. He stretched forward with all his might to grab it, to bring it back, but it— she—was simply gone. To Heaven or to Hell? David knew the answer now. She was in Hell for what she'd done, what she'd brought into the world of men. No, no, no. David sobbed helplessly at the flood of images of his sweet, kind mother, tortured and tormented. Just for him, just for having the hubris to bring him to life.

Surais grinned darkly, sucking in the misery like a fucking milkshake through a straw. "And then your stepfather, well... He wasn't exactly a knight in shining armour."

The smell of stale liquor on foul breath, the backs of giant hands colliding with tender flesh over imaginary infractions. David felt so small again, so defenseless, the man's huge silhouette filling the door to his room, blocking the light from the hall. "Please don't do that again," David whispered, but the man never listened. He just took David by the head or by the hand and used him to find his own fleeting, repulsive release. The man left David dirty, bent over a toilet and violently vomiting up dinner, at least until the boy learned Not to Care. Only right now, in this place, he cared very much.

"And your lovely sister, Saoirse. How sad when the two of you got bullied at school. Did no one come to your aid?" Surais giggled, digging in deeper and twisting the knife even though he had David on his knees.

Blonde ringlets matted with blood from a thrown rock. A tall, strong, very young girl trying her best to launch herself at her attackers, only to be held back by her skinny, desperate big brother. Even then, so very young, David was always thinking of the big picture. She was always the one to leap in, unafraid and uninterested in his cautions. This time, though, there were six of them, boys and girls, and the smallest one was bigger than she was. Even working together, the two of them would lose this fight, lose it badly, and how angry would her father be if they inconvenienced him with a trip to hospital? David hated himself for saying it, but it worked, and she backed off, shaking in his arms. No, he answered her, leading her away with a backward glance at the group. No, it wasn't fair at all.

This was obviously all just too delicious. Surais grinned and put down the dagger, supremely confident in his victory, his utter power over the man in front of him. "And then your priest found out what was happening, and you both got taken away. You must have thought you were safe in the orphanage. Tsk. You weren't though. The men in black made sure of that."

The overripe incense filled his head, made him lighter, less real, less present, but the stone was like ice on his bare flesh. The candles set around the altar should be warm, he thought, shuddering as the man on top of him climbed down and another took his place. But they weren't. The flames should be warm. They would hurt Saoirse. They said. They said it didn't matter what they did to him, since he was just a very smart doll made of blood and guts and blasphemy. He had no soul. The incense turned foul in his nostrils, and he shook his head against the rough stone. Apparently, he wasn't allowed to float away. No, he had to be here for every single moment.

"And when they cut into you..."

The pain was unimaginable. They were not skilled, his butchers, his holy men. Their carvings were not lovely. What they were...what they were was bitterly effective. David didn't know what they were doing. They were so careful not to speak in front of him, so diligent that he remain ignorant of what he was beyond the word "abomination." What they'd done to him before, the agony of it, was nothing compared to this. The life ran out of him, the fragile sense of self, the biggest and most beautiful mysteries of his soul. There would be nothing for him but this, it seemed. Rooms like this, men like this, pain like this. When it passed, finally, they dumped him unceremoniously on a narrow bed in a locked wing of the infirmary. He could hear the children laughing and playing outside his one tiny high window. It was day. When had he gone into that room? It didn't matter, did it? He wasn't a child anymore.

"No, you weren't. You were a tool. A weapon. And you were so, so very good at it, even when it took away your will to live." Surais was having an easy time of it. If he wasn't careful, he'd eat himself into a coma.

It was the little boy, Giacomo. There was nothing special about the boy, about the case, except that it was the case that broke him. It was losing Giacomo that put David on his knees,

151

arms opened up in vertical slashes, the bright blood oddly pretty against the dark stone of the exorcism chamber. His chamber. Sometimes, the demons won. Not often, not on his watch, but sometimes...sometimes they stole souls and lives and no matter how hard he fought, he lost. And when he lost, people died. Children died. All his cleverness, come down to this. A dead child, and the sight of his heart pumping his life's blood out of his arms. He'd already passed out when the cleanup team arrived, acted quickly, saved the abomination's life. It still had its uses, it would seem, although occasionally it failed.

"You poor thing. They did love calling you 'it' when they made you do so many filthy things. Do you think it was really losing Giacomo that made you try to kill yourself, or was it all of the abuse? Do you know? What I want to know, dear David, is what you bear the most guilt over. I want to know about Rhian, and her father."

David shrank down deeper into his ball, wrapped his wings tighter around himself.

That night. God, that night. A woman, heavily pregnant and refusing his help with every ounce of her energy, even as the pain of labor came upon her. She wasn't possessed, she insisted, she was wide-awake, and what was he going to do about that? Her screams echoed off stone walls, and there was so much blood. David didn't know what to do; it was coming in great gouts, pumped out into a slick pool where he knelt, trying to find the babe, hoping it was descended low enough that he could just grab it and pull it out. But it wasn't. The bleeding suddenly stopped, and the woman was dead. In a moment's sickening decision, he took his knife and cut, oh so carefully, along the bottom of her swollen belly, trying to find the infant before it, too, died.

The infant should die. It was an abomination, too.

David cut anyway.

He was elbow deep in blood and tissue when he found the tiny, still form, pulled it forth, and cut the cord. A girl. A girl with golden eyes staring at him from out of the blood and vernix covering her face. A girl daring him to save her life.

David stripped off his cassock and used it to clean her off, rubbing at her chest until she gave out a mighty cry. And that was the moment he knew; this, they would not take from him. He was finished.

"You weren't done. You weren't close to done. The things you did, to keep that child safe…tsk tsk tsk. Such dire sins. Good thing you have no soul to corrupt." Surais grinned wider. Wider than he should be able to grin.

He'd stumbled into the small flat he shared with Saoirse in Rome, the baby still wrapped in black cloth, and his sister, bless her, had just…accepted. Accepted her brother as he was, accepted this strange, motherless child. She was the bright angel in his life, his only link to Heaven. But he wasn't really done. He knew what he had to do. The following night he was back in his workroom, a contract meticulously constructed on curling parchment, using the child's blood to cast a summoning. There was no way to know what kind of monster would come to claim the girl, and when Ipos manifested in that room, David didn't know whether to be terrified or grateful or…

"Or aroused. That's what you went with, wasn't it, you little whore?"

Ipos was a handsome creature. Sometimes they were, demons and devils. Sometimes they were so lovely they would break your heart. Those were the most dangerous of all, for they still bore some stamp of their lives before the Fall. At first, Ipos had been implacable, demanding his daughter immediately, but then he'd gripped David by the arms and looked deeply into his blue eyes. Whatever he saw there, he nodded his great head gravely. "You are worthy. But, you understand, there must be an exceptional contract. She is nobility. She is my daughter."

David nodded slowly. "Anything except my sister's life."

"Come now, little one, I am not a barbarian." Ipos shook his head.

"You impregnated a human woman, knowing it would kill her."

"I loved her." He didn't seem to be grieving, but it was impossible to tell in the feline features.

David shook his head, and Ipos released him. "I've already drawn up the contract. If it satisfies you, I will fulfill it in any way you choose."

"I choose you. Your blood, your seed. My seed."

"I..." David had never been humiliated in quite this way before, and it cut him down to the quick. "I may not be able to give you what you want."

"No?" Ipos stroked his human hands up David's arms, leaving gooseflesh in their wake. "I think you will give me exactly what I want."

"Poor David. Not able to get it up. Well, why should you? No one wants that, no one cares for your pleasure. Except that once." Surais crouched in front of David and moved the furled wings aside until he could see the Nephilim's stricken face. "That's better. Now tell me about your shame."

David fought against it. He did. As if it ultimately mattered. As if it didn't make him a hopeless sinner. But how can an abomination sin without a soul? So many thoughts swirled in his head, a helpless muddle of confusion, mute disbelief, and yes, shame. So much shame. His body may be scarred and worn, but at least it had always been under his command when he needed it to be. Ipos was stripping that from him.

The chamber was cold. It was always cold so far down, but Ipos's hands were like flickers of flame on his skin. David stood so still, back so rigid it was likely to snap, and the demon just laughed. "Oh, David," he purred, standing behind the man, snaking his hand around a slim hip, the words sliding into his ears like honey on velvet. "You're trying so hard, aren't you? But you don't know, do you, how to be what I need you to be right now."

"What do you need from me, Ipos?" David's voice was hushed but laced through with pain and the anguish that he might not be good enough to save Rhian.

"I need you to feel. Just feel." Ipos scraped the nape of David's neck gently with his fangs, leaving no visible marks for all that David felt the jolt of it deep in his belly. He was surprised when a moan escaped his lips. What was this feeling? It was terrifying; it was exhilarating. It was all he could think about—the demon's hands on his body, huge and claw-tipped, urging him to respond.

And he did. God help him, he did. Ipos's hands were skilled, his tongue broad and rough and applied just so, and soon enough, David was writhing under him, making noises he would never have expected to come out of his mouth. Whimpers, mewls. His hands gripped the stone, and his knees were getting bruised, but there was no brutality there. Just knowing touches and hot little growls and purrs of encouragement.

At the absolute last moment, Ipos bit his shoulder, blood and seed mingling on the parchment beneath their writhing bodies. David was in shock, shaking, cold and cored out, and not remotely certain what had just happened to him. Ipos left him there, on the floor, with one last nuzzle to the side of his face, the contract in hand. Shame rushed in to fill the void, with teeth and claws and all-consuming fire. Never again.

Surais grinned and touched David. With a mocking gentleness, he lifted David's face from where his chin was tucked in against his neck, wiping at tears with slimy fingers. "You were lying to yourself though, weren't you? All it took was one handsome Huntsman and you were falling all over yourself to get him in you. Slut."

David shuddered away from the word in his mind, trying to hide from it although it echoed and bounced, and he tried so hard to resist it. *Slut, slut, slut.* He was, yes, but Dallan was good. A good man.

"Your Dallan must be a desperate old man to court a used-up whore like you. What do you think he would say, if he knew about your demon? Maybe he'd want to have a go at you with the demon. You don't know half of what he's gotten up to in his life." Surais reached back and slapped David then, as hard as he could, sending the Nephilim's head rocking.

"S-stop." Something inside David, rabid and feral, came crawling out from under its well-buried rock when Surais talked about Dallan. His head was ringing, and that slap had been a tactical mistake. It was clearing the fog out of his mind, lifting him up from his morass of shame and self-loathing. He'd been a child. He'd been doing his best. He'd fought as hard as he could. He'd experienced pleasure once. These things were not shameful.

Surais slapped him again. David felt his lip split, tasted hot, coppery blood. The heat of it warmed him, gave him something to focus on in the midst of his roiling emotions. "You're nothing but a cheap whore, and the second Dallan Jaeger sees you for what you are, he'll run from you like the plague. You think just because he *said* he loves you, he means it? You think that's real?"

Did Surais really just insult Dallan's *honor*? His *word*? Anger flared from deep within the maelstrom in his mind, with rage following when anger just wasn't a strong enough emotion. How could this creature possibly dare impugn Dallan's honor? The man's Oath was one thing that David found himself believing in, even when he didn't believe in himself. Even when he believed he was worthless. Even as his faith in his God waned. Dallan was a man who kept his word.

"You don't get to say his name." There was a subtle silver-blue flash of light as the cut lip healed. His blade was concealed by his wings, dropped under Surais' vicious onslaught. His fingers slipped comfortably around the hilt.

Surais' eyes narrowed as he finally started to get the hint that he'd overstepped, miscalculated on a grand scale. "I say what I please, and you have fed me very well. Now, it's time to put you down." His hand flexed, razor-sharp claws clacking against each other as he lunged forward to swipe them across David's throat.

The lunge ended with the tip of David's sword sliding effortlessly deep into Surais' rotted heart. David pushed through the chest cavity, not stopping until the hilt hit, flush with the creature's chest. Shaky knees barely held him up as he stood, looking down on the body and feeling decidedly lost. How would he find his way home?

One thing did seem certain. He had to make sure this monster was well and truly dead, unable to rear his ugly head again. David reached down and grabbed a fistful of oily hair and lifted Surais up, sword parting head from neck in a clean, vicious swipe. Now that ugly head was his, and he threw it unceremoniously against the far wall.

He was just pulling his armor on when the heavy stone door, invisible from the inside and sealed from the outside, opened to reveal Dallan, several members of the Hunt, and a handful of what appeared to be dark-haired elves like something out of the books he read to the children.

Dallan stared at him, the relief on his face so clear David had to smile.

"Hello, *minn ástir*," David said.

Chapter Fifteen

David looked across the chamber at Dallan and the crowd behind him, shifting his weight from one foot to another until Dallan took a step toward him. That was all he needed to rush forward and throw his arms around Dallan, so glad to see him that he was shaking despite himself. Dallan squeezed him so hard that his ribs creaked, and David wrapped his wings around them both instinctively.

"Is..." David began, murmuring into the man's neck.

"Oscar's safe, love. We have him. Other than one turncoat, all the Sluagh are dead," Dallan finished before David could get the question past his lips.

"I thought I'd never see you again. I thought you couldn't get into Faerie." The words were still muffled by Dallan's body, since David refused to let him go.

"When we realised what had happened, that Surais *took* you, we dragged our one prisoner up to the boundaries and demanded an audience with the king. He was none too pleased with Surais' usurping of power, so he gave us passage and an escort." Dallan finally pulled away, searching David's face. "I thought I'd lost you, when I'd just barely found you."

"Surais was very powerful. It was...a near thing. But then he made the biggest mistake he could make. He spoke ill of you." It was enough to break the spell, to set him free, and not just from Surais' power. From a lifetime of guilt and pain and shame. "I want to tell you everything."

"And I want to hear whatever it is you have to say, my love, but let's get out of here and figure out what to do with Oscar first." Dallan forced himself to step away.

"He's still unconscious? I think that I can manipulate his memories and heal him. He never has to know." David's tone was hopeful, because while he knew he could do those things, he wasn't at all sure they were the right things.

Dallan nodded, and after David folded his wings back and sheathed his sword, they left that room together. It was underneath an abandoned temple on the edge of a marsh, not far at all from the borderlands of Faerie. "I was so close the whole time," David murmured incredulously. "But I felt like I was a million miles from you."

"Never, *minn ástir*. You will never be that far from me." Even if they were in different worlds, or continents apart. They refused to part hands as they met up with the rest of the Hunt, who had Oscar on a pallet. His color was pale, and he had a myriad of small wounds crisscrossing his body, but he looked whole.

David knelt beside him and stroked the hair back from his face. "Ah, love. I am so very sorry. We'll make it right for you, I swear," he whispered, only for Dallan's ears.

"You'd best be going," the captain of the escort announced, looking up at the placement of the moon to tell the time. "His Majesty gave you until dawn to travel his lands in peace."

"Right. Please convey to him our most humble thanks for assisting us in ridding both our worlds of this plague." Dallan picked Oscar up off the pallet and handed him to M'baza before climbing up on his warhorse and taking the boy up in front of him.

"I shall do so. Now it is time to leave." The warning was clear, and the alliance uneasy.

David unfurled his wings and took to the air, finding it both impossible that this was only his second time flying and unthinkable that he wasn't just falling out of the sky. "I'll follow you home."

The Hunt took off for the border, which, like so many things in the Twist, was deceptively close. David thought that just maybe Dallan had the ability to manipulate distance here as he did in the mundane world, because they reached the shimmery, slightly sick-making border in just a few minutes of hard riding. It took some courage to follow the Hunt through the barrier, but other than a few moments of disorientation, there were no ill effects. They emerged in the forest where they'd left, a bare half an hour from home. Only a few hours had passed, and that seemed as unlikely as the rest of the horrible, extraordinary night.

In a few more minutes, they were all crowding the small beach out back of David and Saoirse's home, the horses and hounds kicking up the damp sand. Dallan shifted Oscar in his lap. "Alexander, take the boy while I get down." David wondered if the compactly built blond in the Greek Aegis breastplate was in truth Alexander the Great. If it looked like a famous world conqueror holding his foster son, then chances were that was exactly who Alexander was.

The warrior looked at David and smiled, holding Oscar's weight as though it were nothing. "It is unfortunate that the Hunt Master has claimed you." Dark eyes sparkled mischievously, flirtatiously.

No power in either world could stop David from blushing, but when he looked for that instinctive revulsion inside him, he didn't find it. He was actually able to return the smile, albeit with a tinge of the exhaustion weighing down his muscles. "And yet thoroughly claimed is what I am."

"I have never seen him like this, and I have known him for ages," Alexander teased as Dallan came in between them to take Oscar back.

"He already knows I'm an utter fool for him, no need to rub it in," the Hunt Master teased right back.

David found himself laughing, almost in relief. This was good. This was right. He put his wings away, traded the armor for the clothes he was wearing before he changed, and watched as Dallan bid farewell to the Hunt. Promises were made to come to the Twist more often, and to bring David, who could clearly use a holiday.

When the last baying hound had disappeared across the sea into the Twist, Dallan and David made their way back to the house. That short walk felt like a voyage to the exhausted pair, and David saw that Dallan was also flagging. Saoirse was waiting at the back door, and from the circles beneath her eyes she'd been waiting there all night, a blanket wrapped around her. When she saw them struggle up the last few feet of the path and come through the gate, she rushed them, dropping the blanket in her haste to throw her arms around them all.

"Thank God, thank God," she said over and over, kissing David on the cheek, then Dallan, then Oscar, then all three of them over again. "I was afraid none of you were coming back to me."

"We're here, sis, we're all here, and we're all right." David smiled and wrapped an arm around his sister's shoulders when she moved to pick up the blanket to cover Oscar.

"Oscar, too?"

"Oscar, too, although there's work yet to be done for him," Dallan murmured, shifting the boy's weight in his arms. "Let's get him up to bed."

David caught Dallan's eyes, full of questions. To let him remember, or to spare him? Spare him, most assuredly. Perhaps it was not their decision to make, but they were making it anyway. The trio tried to be as quiet as possible in the predawn gloom, carrying Oscar up the stairs to his small room. The space was crammed with posters, mostly from Broadway musicals, and a messily made bed with a bright violet duvet. David pulled the covers back, and Dallan laid the boy down at last. Saoirse got him a pair of pajama pants, and she and David got him dressed.

"Saoirse, we need to take care of a few things. Would you mind giving us a few moments?" David didn't want to kick her out, but Saoirse didn't like watching him do magic either.

"Right. I'll just go put on the kettle, then." The universal remedy for any situation, magical or mundane. She left them standing shoulder to shoulder next to Oscar's bed.

"He can't remember this. It would destroy his world, just when it's starting." David sat carefully on the very edge of the bed.

"Agreed." Dallan rested his hand on David's shoulder as if magnetically drawn there. "You can heal all the small cuts and bruises, and you can take away the memory. But there's one thing that needs to happen."

"Hm?" David closed his eyes and stroked his thumb over Oscar's forehead, concentrating, the wounds fading first to faint lines, and then into oblivion.

"He'll need to have a terrible nightmare. We'll be right here for him, but the memory can't just be walled away. It has to be experienced, if only in a dream, or it will haunt him. You can't truly steal a memory."

How David wished they could. He opened his eyes, looked at Dallan, and nodded, heart heavy. "I understand. We'll be right here," he reiterated, closing his eyes again and pushing back into Oscar's mind. It was surprisingly easy to find the memories and dim them, almost like using a tool in a graphic design program. Blur, fade. Now a gentle nudge to move Oscar into a normal sleep, another to bring the dream to the forefront of his mind.

He backed off when Oscar started to whimper, grabbing Dallan's hand as he forced himself to wait, watching the distress play out on Oscar's young face. Dallan gripped his hand tightly, and David could feel that rock-steady support bracing him.

"When?" David whispered.

"Soon, love," Dallan answered.

"Nonononono..." Oscar whimpered, eyes darting back and forth from behind his eyelids, until suddenly they shot open and he sat up, breathing hard. David immediately came forward, settling his hand on Oscar's shoulder, and then finding himself pulled into a close hug.

"It was a bad dream, love... Dallan and I heard you and came up here to check on you. Just a bad dream." David found the lies distressingly easy.

"It felt so real." Oscar let go to look at his arms, searching for evidence of the cuts and finding none. "There were monsters, David."

"Not in this house, there weren't," David stressed, sitting back and cupping the boy's face. "You are safe here. Always. Dallan and I will make sure of that."

"I know. I do." Finally, Oscar's breathing returned to normal, and he curled back into his covers.

"Are you going to be all right, sweetheart?" Dallan asked.

"Yeah...thank you." Oscar smiled faintly, as the dream fled in the dawning light. "Just still so sleepy." Even as he nodded off, he looked blearily up at them. "I got the part."

David didn't have to fake his answering smile. "Of course you did, sweetheart. Get some rest, and we'll be here to talk later if you need us." After their own much-needed sleep.

Downstairs, each gratefully took a mug of tea and leaned against the counter. "It was a near thing, Saoirse. But he's all right. He thinks it was all a dream."

His sister nodded, blonde curls in disarray. "I asked Jen if she would mind coming over in a couple of hours to watch the little ones. Apparently we've had a stomach bug rip through the house, and they were the only ones who escaped it."

"Good idea. I'd say we all need a hell of a lie-in." Dallan wrapped his arm around David's shoulder, and David leaned in to press his face to the side of his neck, breathing in his scent.

"Or something." Saoirse's eyes sparkled as she took her tea to the living room sofa to wait for Jen.

"Or something," her brother agreed.

"David…" Dallan pulled David into a crushing embrace.

"I need you. I'm tired of not knowing. I'm tired of being scared." The words were muffled against Dallan's neck, but he understood perfectly.

"Surais, did he…"

"Torture me, belittle me. Drag out all my worst memories and make me relive them. Hell, he disemboweled me." David swallowed hard, anger the only emotion that litany of abuse produced, and wasn't that a nice surprise?

"Gods. David, you need time. Time to heal, time to…"

"No. I don't need time. I could almost thank him. When he finally pushed me too far, I didn't break. I stopped crying. I got angry." He pulled back, looked at Dallan. "And I realised that what I need is you. I need to know what you feel like. I need to know what love feels like. I'm sick and tired of that being taken away from me, over and over. That David is dead, died in that chamber, and this David wants you very, very badly."

"I think at this point what we need is privacy. And showers. And then to see what happens." David was like a giant walking nerve, and he could hear the hesitancy in Dallan's voice, feel it in the gentle way Dallan took his hand and led him toward the stairs. For now, all David did was nod his agreement. But if Dallan thought he was going to get off the hook with a shower and a cuddle, he had another thing coming.

Once inside David's room with the door closed, he turned to

Dallan. "Would you mind if I went first?"

Dallan plopped tiredly down on the chair in the corner. "Go right ahead, love." He then proceeded to make a choked little noise when David stripped down right in front of him. No provocation this time, no dares or pushing. Just that newly healed flesh revealed, and he wasn't trying to hide. "Is it all right, finally, to say you're beautiful?"

David found a smile. "If that's honestly what you think, then say it. No more leaving, no more running."

"Then you're the most exquisite sight I've ever beheld, *minn ástir*, and I could look at you every day for the rest of our lives." Dallan's voice was hushed. It was the reverence you paid to the divine.

"I still think you're blind, but...I love that you think so." David bit his lower lip and ducked into the bathroom. He showered quickly and came back out just as naked as when he went in, toweling his damp hair. The towel found its way into the laundry hamper, and he crawled under the duvet, shivering against the early morning chill in the air.

Dallan stripped out of his own clothing with the same no-nonsense practicality and ease that he'd shown in the forest with Nynia, only this time David was unabashedly staring at the strong, sturdy body, the muscled chest, even Dallan's half-hard cock. "Trust you finally got your eyeful?" Dallan teased.

"This time." David grinned and pulled the duvet up to burrow in while Dallan went to shower. Even though he was exhausted, falling asleep was the farthest thing from his mind, and when Dallan came back out with a jar of hand cream, all he could do was lift up the duvet. "It's freezing. Get in here."

The skin-on-skin slide of Dallan's body against his was enough to make him gasp, and it was David that kissed Dallan first. He was still not practiced with kissing, and it felt so intimate when Dallan pressed him to the mattress and nuzzled his lips apart, tasting deeper. Again, they let themselves get lost in the act, in the simple but profound connection of shared breaths and slow stroking hands.

"I never imagined this," David whispered against Dallan's lips.

"You don't have to imagine, love. I'm right here, and I've got you." David couldn't conceive of a safer place in this or any other world. Dallan's mouth left his at last as he kissed and licked a slow path down David's neck. David's breathing came harder, and his hips shifted as he went fully hard so fast his head spun a little. He clasped at Dallan's bicep, and reached around his waist, holding him close with his other hand. "Mmm. Gods, you taste good."

"Tell me." What did an angel taste like exactly?

"Like petrichor, like lightning in the broken sky, flavours mere humans weren't meant to know," Dallan whispered, the words small gusts of air over David's waiting lips.

"Dallan, God...more?" There was an ache in him, a clench of muscle and need and emptiness that was just too much to bear. An ache that only Dallan inside him could banish.

"More...always, love. Always more for you." Dallan's mouth found one small, pink nipple, teeth scraping over the tight, hard bud of flesh delicately before suckling it, almost overloading David's system when Dallan slid a confident hand around his straining prick.

The sound David made then was not remotely dignified, but if Dallan's answering moan was any indication, it was entirely appropriate. David found himself spreading his thighs, tugging at Dallan until Dallan was on top of him, weighing him down before he just flew away. "Want you inside me. Need it...Dallan." He wouldn't beg, because he didn't need to beg. Dallan, this extraordinary man, was his. All his. Forever.

"Gods, yes...fuck, David." Yes, that...fuck. Now. Dallan

fumbled with the hand cream, slicked up his fingers. David couldn't stop shaking, not with fear, but with the sheer, overwhelming complexity of feelings, physical and emotional, when Dallan slid a finger inside him.

It was an invasion. Of course it was. But it also felt right, like he'd been too empty for too long, waiting for the one person he could trust enough to do this. To open him up, to press one and then two fingers deep until the faint burn was a delightful stretch. Another finger, and he was sure. "That's enough. God, Dallan, enough. Want you now." The delicious tension had him on the bleeding edge already, and he'd be damned if he let go this soon, without feeling Dallan inside him properly.

"Yeah? You nice and open for me?" his lover whispered, moving his fingers and finding a place inside him that made David cry out, his hips shooting right off the bed.

"Yes, yes, oh God, come *on*!" Because that just wasn't fair play, now, was it?

Dallan stroked his slick hand over his cock and pressed his forehead to David's. "Mine, *minn ástir*. Always." That connection calmed David just enough to take a deep breath. "Push down, sweetheart." When he did, Dallan pressed forward, and in one drawn-out, oh-so-slow glide he was there, finally, exactly where David needed him to be.

They were both shaking by this point, and Dallan snagged another blanket, not moving inside David yet, letting him get used to the feeling, wrapping them up close against the chill and their own impossible need. Their world was the bed, their cocoon, and who knew what might emerge now that there were no barriers between them.

Something new, something different. Something better.

David wrapped his legs around Dallan's hips, his eyes wide, pupils blown. "Dallan." He needed something, but he wasn't sure what.

Dallan moved his hips, just a few inches, out and then in, and then David knew. What he needed was for Dallan to *take*. "More more more," he murmured against Dallan's lips, feeling his smile more than seeing it.

"More. Gods, yes." The rhythm Dallan set was primal, old as time but new as this bright morning to David, who'd known nothing but brutality and practicality and force applied in many and varied ways. There was no force here, just two people trying to messily, hopelessly shove themselves together into one whole being.

Dallan changed his angle and found that sweet spot inside David again, and again, and in the end it was too much. David might have wanted this joining to go on forever, but it couldn't, not when Dallan did *that*. His body arched and twisted and the pleasure was so much more than that, it was ecstasy, the kind that he'd spent years in the priesthood unsuccessfully chasing. The ecstatic divine—how could you find it if you were an abomination?

Now the abomination knew where it had been hiding all along—in the body of a patient man who was buried deep inside him. David stroked his hands up and down Dallan's broad back as his own orgasm claimed him, wracked him. His Dallan. There was nothing else.

When they'd ridden out the storm, Dallan turned onto his back and pulled David into his arms, where he wriggled until he found the perfect spot on Dallan's chest to rest his head, feeling Dallan smile tiredly against his hair. "I didn't know."

"But now you do." Dallan made sure the blankets were tucked around David's shoulders. "And we can have it any way we like, forever."

"I'm very sleepy," David announced, his voice slurring a little.

"Then rest, *minn ástir*. You've worked so very hard. And come so very far."

David knew that he would have to go back to work tomorrow morning. There was still a copycat to catch and criminals who never rested. That world seemed very far away from the world of this bed and his lover and the reality they'd created between them. He quieted his thoughts and burrowed in closer to Dallan.

The slanting morning light across the bed was a simple benediction, a complex promise.

About the Author

L.A. is a professional writer finally crossing over into fiction. She has a background in the Classics and Religious Studies, and those themes will come up again and again in her work. L.A. lives in Texas, has two incredible kids, and a varying number of rescue mutts. Reach out to her on Twitter; she'd love to hear from you!

Email: lethaswicker@gmail.com
Website: lastockman.wordpress.com
Twitter: @la_stockman
Facebook: facebook.com/LAStockman

NineStar Press, LLC

www.ninestarpress.com

www.ingramcontent.com/pod-product-compliance
Lightning Source LLC
Chambersburg PA
CBHW050942120626
46552CB00001B/332